Sherlock Holmes and the Lyme Regis Legacy

By

David Ruffle

Paperback ISBN 9781780921006
ePub ISBN 9781780921013
PDF ISBN 9781780921020

Published in the UK by MX Publishing
335 Princess Park Manor, Royal Drive, London, N11 3GX
www.mxpublishing.com

Cover layout and construction by
www.staunch.com

Dedicated to the 'four'

Ayden, Kieron, Nikiah and Deryn

And to the people of Lyme Regis, *past present and future.*

Contents:

After fortuitously coming across an unpublished manuscript detailing a visit to Lyme Regis made by Sherlock Holmes and Dr Watson that was apparently written by Watson himself, I busied myself both during the editing and pre-publication stage of this tale with trying to find documentary evidence that the events Watson (published as *'Sherlock Holmes and the Lyme Regis Horror'*) described actually occurred. If I could find such evidence it would bolster my already firm conviction that this account was indeed one written by Watson.

The manuscript detailed, amongst other things, how a certain Mrs Heidler owned a boarding-house where Holmes and Watson stayed, so one of the starting points in my research was to track down any present day Heidlers; Heidler being an unusual enough surname I thought I may get some joy there. I did enter into some correspondence with a family in Cornwall, but they had no knowledge of anyone connected to the events in the book, nor indeed did they have any connection to Lyme Regis that they were aware of. That was the way things stood as *'Sherlock Holmes and the Lyme Regis Horror'* was published in December 2009.

In the late summer of 2011 I received a message via email from a Derek Heidler in High Wycombe who informed me that his grandfather was a Nathaniel Heidler who was born in 1881 and died in 1974; his marriage certificate showed his marriage to an Elizabeth Hill of Lyme Regis in April 1901. This was a result indeed and news that I had long given up on; namely, proof that at least some of the account must have indeed been correct. There was another surprise in store for me; along with the wealth of information in subsequent emails that Derek sent me regarding Nathaniel's later life, he also told me of a tin trunk that contained mementos and paperwork pertaining to Nathaniel's army career and business dealings plus more personal items. Derek set to work on my behalf sifting through these testaments and reminders of his grandfather's life. About a month after we first corresponded he rang me with some exciting news; he had found what appeared to be notes drawn up by Watson of a further case in Lyme Regis. These he duly sent to me; the notes were comprehensive, but for all that, just notes. However, along with this bundle of notes was a sizeable sheaf of paper, neatly folded in two and inserted into this bundle. This turned out to be an account prepared from these scribbling as if in readiness for publication. The handwriting was the very same as on the manuscript I already had in possession, but as to why Watson never worked these notes up in complete form for publication, I do have some idea; towards the end of this adventure there is an incident involving Holmes that I think would have precluded Watson from ever making public this particular action of Holmes, but I will go into that later.

There was also a diary contained in this parcel which Derek had initially assumed to be one kept by his grandfather. Despite it being in his possession, he told me, he had never exercised any great curiosity about it and had only given it the scantest of attention, believing it to be notes for a story rather than a documentation of actual events. It was adorned with an embossed leather cover and apparently ill-used, this journal did not belong to Nathaniel Heidler however, but, to another, but more of that later.

I trust I have not taken too many liberties with Watson's words and have completed this tale in a manner that he would have approved of. My own interpolations are actually few and far between; the chief difficulty lay in the fact that Watson's handwriting was notoriously hard to decipher as many have found before me.

As in 'The Lyme Regis Horror' I have added a few pieces of my own featuring Holmes and Watson plus Lyme Regis in various vignettes, drabbles, odd tales, flights of fancy and I have also included a short history of Lyme Regis for those who wish to know just a little more about the setting for some of these tales.

But, before we can head off to that 'pearl of the Dorset coast', , we must first find our way once more to 221b Baker Street...................where two old friends await us.

David Ruffle December2011

Chapter One

The rays of the autumn sun had been busy spreading their colour and warmth throughout the dreariest of London streets, bringing them to life as though they were reborn. Even a vast city of alleyways, thoroughfares and lanes such as London became animate as a result of nature's munificence. This gift that nature so richly bestowed was absorbed into the very fabric of the many edifices. Grey, nondescript buildings became honeyed, softened and radiant as the sun struck them. Although I often yearned for the shingle of Southsea, the glades of the New Forest or the beauty of Dorset, I would be the first to concede that the city had a beauty of its own.

This particular period of fine weather was a most welcome antidote for the dismal summer we had endured. Even this singular outpouring of Mother Nature's bounties had failed to lift the spirits of my friend, Mr Sherlock Holmes. He had been in a black depression since our return from Norfolk where we had looked into the singular problem of the 'Dancing Men' that so profoundly affected Mrs Elsie Cubitt and ultimately resulted in the death of her beloved and devoted husband, Mr Hilton Cubitt of Ridling Thorpe Manor.

I was busy the afternoon of which I write, compiling my notes of the case which will no doubt appear at some point in the memoirs of my remarkable friend, whilst he sat curled up in the basket chair staring at the ceiling with no word passing his lips until he suddenly sprang to his feet and hovered over me.

"So you intend, Watson to publish an account of my utter failure to prevent the death of my client, Hilton Cubitt?"

"You will excuse me I am sure if I do not see it that way."

"What other way, pray tell, is there to see it?"

"Holmes, you have no reason to reproach yourself. You did all that you could have possibly done. And remember, it was you who deciphered the code and laid the trap which netted Abe Slaney."

"I should have foreseen the danger and acted sooner, instead of which a noble gentleman lies dead," Holmes spat out, bringing his clenched fist down hard on the edge of his armchair.

"Death and destruction visited the Cubitt family in the guise of Abe Slaney. He and he alone is to blame, not you, Holmes."

"I know your words are meant to salve, Watson, but the sad truth is that they do not. I will go to my room rather than inflict any more of my miserable company on you. I do not wish to be disturbed even if the Premier and his entire cabinet were to come calling, I am not at home."

I knew it was futile to remonstrate with Holmes when he slipped into these black depths which opened up and swallowed him. Seventeen years ago he had given me prior warning of these moods that would descend upon him from time to time. It was when there was a lack of meaningful cases for him to apply his unique talents that the blackness came upon him, which unfortunately these days was more and more often. Regretfully, on these occasions he was prone to use artificial stimulation by way of a seven percent solution of cocaine, despite my repeated attempts to wean him off it completely. This fiend of addiction was only sleeping and I was acutely aware that this sleep could be disturbed at any time.

There was no telling when this particular mood would pass and as I was of no practical help to my friend, I whiled away a few hours planning a forthcoming trip to Lyme Regis. I had paid my first visit to that delightful town two years previously in the late spring of 1896, in the company of Holmes. Whilst there, we had encountered an adversary unlike any other we had known. It is, however, a story for which the world is not yet prepared and although I have written an account of all that occurred, it is not intended for publication, a state of affairs which I believe is unlikely ever to change.

In the midst of the peril that we found ourselves in, I formed an attachment to a certain lady in the town and my feelings of deep affection were joyously reciprocated. Mrs Beatrice Heidler is the lady's name and since then I have spent as much time in Lyme Regis as I possibly could, which even so is rather less than she or I would like.

I could hear occasional mournful notes, although perhaps abstract scrapings would describe them best, coming from Holmes's violin as I penned a letter to Beatrice, setting a date in October for my next visit. Holmes took these absences of mine in his stride; in some ways I felt I had become a fixture for him much in the same way as his shag tobacco, the old black pipe and the index books. I did not doubt

2

his friendship, but all the same I had become an institution, an integral part of Holmes's life and truth be told I was not displeased at this. Holmes was a man of narrow and fixed habits and I accepted that at times I would only exist on the periphery of his life, yet we had a bond which transcended any petty squabbles or differences which reared their heads on occasion. We were in many ways dependent upon each other, even Holmes I believed would acknowledge the truth of that.

There was no sign of Holmes the following morning, his bedroom door remained firmly closed and the enticing aroma of bacon, eggs and freshly brewed coffee did nothing to tempt him from his private sanctum. I felt sure he was awake and possibly had been so all night; any kind of failure even if it was coupled with eventual success was anathema to him. Mrs Hudson was busying herself ferrying the remains of a fine breakfast down to the scullery when Holmes's door finally opened.

"Watson, I fear I owe you an apology. I was a touch short with you yesterday evening, but this latest incident in Norfolk has helped to make up my mind on a matter which has been on my mind for some considerable time. It is my intention to retire from this position I have created for myself."

"You are surely not serious, Holmes?"

"Very much so. New advances in science are making my position untenable. Soon, all these advances will be available to every police force in the country and the days of the gifted amateur will be over. The skills I have sought to master will become increasingly irrelevant. Mechanical and technological progressions will alter forever the working patterns and the lives of all of us and I do not have the energy or indeed the inclination to keep up with whatever the 20th century may throw our way. Retirement it is at some point in the near future, my friend."

"I urge you to reconsider. In my view, your singular and unique gifts are as much in need today as they have ever been and I see no sign of that changing in the foreseeable future."

"There is another reason too, Watson."

"And what may that be?" I asked of him.

"You are about to desert me once again for a wife. The only signs of selfishness I can ever recall in our long association have revolved around your dalliances with the fairer sex."

3

"Holmes, you know full well the situation regarding Mrs Heidler and me. We have no plans to wed before her son attains his majority which is a full three years away so there are no immediate plans to desert you as you put it. Besides, where will you go, what will you do?"

"As to where, there is no mystery; I have already taken steps to purchase a villa on the Sussex downs near Fulworth Cove. It is secluded and as far away from the madding crowd as possible. There, I intend to spend my final days in the guise of a bee keeper. Fascinating creatures, bees, don't you think, Watson?"

"I have to say, Holmes, that I have given the subject of bees very little thought."

"You should endeavour to do so for I tell you we have much to learn from them. I will also while away my time by compiling a book which will encompass the whole art of detection and deduction into a single volume although I do find myself questioning the usefulness of such a tome in this modern world."

"But, Holmes, the cases still continue to come your way. Scotland Yard still has reason to consult you. You have so much to give."

"Cases may come my way, but they are not the *great* cases of yesteryear. I fritter away whatever talents I may possess on criminals with no imagination and no ingenuity. My very existence is rapidly becoming stale and I abhor the commonplace of existence with all my soul as you well know."

We said no more about the matter that day. I was fully expecting for Holmes to have had a change of heart, but nothing seemed to deter him from the course on which he was set. I enlisted the aid of Inspector Lestrade; I positively encouraged the man to come round in the evenings and relate any particular problems he was grappling with. None triggered off any great interest in Holmes although he did give Lestrade one or two pointers as to their solution and I had no doubt he would be proved to be right.

I really began to believe that we had seen the last of Mr Sherlock Holmes as the finest consulting detective in the world. The only positive boon to arise from Holmes's decision was that he was no longer in the doldrums. He had a spring in his step and he undertook autumn walks with me in the local parks with a fervency I had never seen before. I was hopeful, therefore, of persuading Holmes to visit Lyme Regis once more.

"Oh no," he replied, "I assure you I have no wish to visit *that* town again, beautiful as it may be. I am more than content to remain in this great city, observing the comings and goings, the choruses and the bleatings of the inhabitants. Besides, who knows, my dear fellow, I may yet find myself with meaningful work to do."

He was not to be persuaded although I tried my best on subsequent occasions and so it was that on the 12th October I found myself at Waterloo, boarding the train to Axminster, a journey which always wakened mixed feelings in me. My initial visit to Lyme so very nearly cost me my life, succeeding visits served to *rejuvenate* my life.

Oct. 11

So, he is coming. His pretty Widow Woman hard at work cleaning Windows. On her Knees scrubbing the Doorstep. If only she Knew. If only He Knew. I must Allow her this Selfless Preparation, after all Cleanliness is next to Godliness and both of them will be Meeting their Maker soon. I will Have Them where I want them And Despatch them.

But now Another demands my Attention. Another who sat in Judgment on Me. As so many have. The Tables will be Turned. He will see. They will see.

Patience. Patience. My ~~goal~~ reward is Near.

Chapter Two

Upon my arrival in Lyme Regis I made my way to Coombe Street where Beatrice, Mrs Heidler, ran a small guest house assisted by her son Nathaniel who had just attained eighteen years. It was painful to be separated from her for weeks at a time, but the reunions were entirely joyous; they went a long way towards assuaging my feelings of sadness at our absences from each other's lives. We looked forward to the time where all our time would be spent together.

For reasons of propriety I did not stay with Beatrice during my visits. Of late I had sojourned with the Coade family in their wonderful home, Belmont House which had breathtaking views down to the Cobb and a garden which was a paradise in itself.

For readers who may not be aware of this construction, the Cobb is a man-made buttress giving protection to the harbour and town from frequent storms. The first written mention of the Cobb was in a 1328 document describing it as having been damaged by storms. The structure was apparently made of oak piles driven into the seabed with boulders stacked between them. The boulders were floated into place tied between empty barrels. A 1685 account describes it as being made of boulders simply heaped up on each other: *"an immense mass of stone, of a shape of a demi-lune, with a bar in the middle of the concave: no one stone that lies there was ever touched with a tool or bedded in any sort of cement, but all the pebbles of the see{sic} are piled up, and held by their bearings only, and the surge plays in and out through the interstices of the stone in a wonderful manner."* The Cobb had been destroyed or severely damaged by storms several times; it was swept away in 1377 which led to the destruction of 50 boats and 80 houses. The southern arm was added in the 1690s, and rebuilt in 1793 following its destruction in a storm the previous year. This is thought to be the first time that mortar was used in the Cobb's construction. The Cobb was reconstructed in 1820 using Portland Admiralty Roach, a type of Portland stone and stands as a stark reminder of the power of nature and mankind's struggle against the elemental forces.

7

For this visit, however, I was to stay with my old friend, Dr Godfrey Jacobs at the house he shared with his wife, Sarah and their three children, Arthur, Cecil and young Violet. They had previously lived in a picturesque, but somewhat cramped cottage in Sherborne Lane which served as both living accommodation and as a surgery for Jacobs's patients to attend. With the birth of their daughter, Violet there came a need to find a larger dwelling. Fortunately an opportunity to acquire a much larger house in Monmouth Street presented itself. The house had the added bonus of extra rooms to be used as a surgery, a dispensary and a comfortable waiting room. The room I boarded in during my visits was at the very top of the house with wonderful views across the churchyard to the sea beyond.

The spell of warm weather we had experienced in London had pleasingly migrated to Dorset and after dropping my luggage at Dr Jacobs's I strolled to and along the seafront in company with Beatrice. The beauty of this part of the world never failed to move me and to have this view affiliated with a most friendly town was eminently agreeable. Residents of the town greeted me as an old friend as we walked the length of the seafront. Especially gratifying was the fact that although everyone knew of my association with Sherlock Holmes, I was accepted, not as some mere appendage of the great detective, but in my own right. The more time I spent in Lyme Regis the more I became convinced that one day this would be my home.

I was lost in this reverie when I felt myself jostled and a gentleman who had collided with me mumbled an apology and disappeared towards the town. I thought nothing of it at the time, but when we had returned to Coombe Street I was astonished to find a semi-crushed butterfly in my coat pocket. The only way it could have found its way there, I reasoned, was for the gentleman who had brushed against me to have placed it there. As to why, I had no answers. Perhaps after all the years spent with Sherlock Holmes I should have had an inkling of what it meant, but to me it was an isolated if not exactly whimsical incident and was soon forgotten.

I was to encounter Dr Jacobs rather earlier than I had expected that evening. Beatrice had presented Nathaniel and me with a splendid meal of oysters, bouillon soup, broiled fish and a delicious plum pudding to round off the meal. I had hardly brought the first spoonful of plum pudding to my mouth when there was an urgent knocking at the door.

8

"Elizabeth for you, Nathaniel? She obviously can't wait to see you," I joked. Elizabeth being Nathaniel's fiancée.

"Watson," exclaimed Jacobs, "sorry to interrupt your evening, but I have just been called out to what has been reported to me as a suspicious death and would welcome your expertise and your experience."

I glanced at Beatrice who nodded her acquiescence albeit with reluctance, a certain amount of trepidation flashing across her features.

"I have not brought any medical paraphernalia with me; I thought it tempting fate a tad too much," I said.

"I have all we need here," Jacobs said, patting his medical bag. "Besides it sounds as though this fellow is beyond all practical help."

I threw on my coat and followed Jacobs out into the quiet of Coombe Street. He turned to the right, walked across the river bridge and into Sherborne Lane, an ancient and narrow track way and although of no great length was one of the steepest climbs in Lyme.

"Where are we heading?" I wheezed.

"Sidmouth Road. All uphill I am afraid, Watson. We are going to Seaview Villa, the home of Robert Fane. He is a local solicitor, although now retired. His general factotum, Joseph, was dispatched to me and I in turn dispatched him to Sergeant Street. Watson, I have to tell you I live in dread of the horror we encountered revisiting this town. The fear I felt then bubbles to the surface in my darkest moments and if this should prove to be a case of history repeating itself......"

"The evil we encountered back then is well and truly no more. I believe we have nothing to fear from that quarter, although, like you I have nightmares still; dark, forbidding dreams which the dawn barely chases away."

Readers, I trust, will forgive one more allusion to this earlier investigation by Holmes and me in Lyme Regis; it is a tale which is entirely unsuitable for this series of sketches and reminiscences, yet being here in Lyme is always a stark reminder of that time no matter how many times I visit. However, it became apparent to me very quickly and forcibly that there was really nowhere I would rather be than this quiet town on the Dorsetshire coast.

Seaview Villa was actually a rather grand house on the favoured western side of Lyme. The door was open and we walked into the darkened hall. The sound of pitiful, heartbreaking sobbing reached our ears and from a door on the right there emerged a statuesque lady, her bright, clear features disfigured by tears and grief. She ran to Jacobs and put her arms around his neck.

"Dr Jacobs, he is in here. Oh Doctor, he looks as though he had met the Devil himself in his death throes. I can't bear to look at him, but I cannot leave him alone in there."

"We are here now, Martha," said Jacobs, taking her hands in his, most tenderly. "This is Dr Watson who has been kind enough to come and lend his assistance. Watson, this is Mrs Martha Doggett who has been Mr Fane's housekeeper for some twenty years."

Mrs Doggett was too anguished to acknowledge my presence in any, but the most cursory fashion. With a visible shudder she led us into what turned out to be Robert Fane's study. The room was extraordinary; every wall adorned with shelves full of books; books even lay on the floor in stacks which seemed to defy gravity in their haste to reach higher and higher. The room spoke of learning, contentment and wealth, but the most extraordinary feature of the room was the figure lying prone on the carpet.

The man was of late middle-age, his face adorned with a black beard of quite massive proportion. His legs were twisted almost to the point of being knotted, his arms stretched out rigidly horizontal to his body with hands tightly clenched. His mouth was open as though screaming out defiance. However death had visited this man, it was a terrible and agonising end. There were no apparent signs of violence to the body and while it was possible that a fatal heart attack had cut down this man, the contortions of his body aroused an instinctive suspicion of foul play.

Jacobs was suggesting to Mrs Doggett that cups of tea all round may be beneficial for all of us and nodding, she left the room. He closed the door after her and his next words confirmed that I was right to harbour these doubts.

"Watson, I am not convinced that we have a death by natural causes here. There is a small amount of froth in the corners of his mouth plus a few specks in his beard; that and the appearance of the body leads me to suspect the use of poison."

"I am inclined to agree with you. The poor man, what agonies he must have gone through."

10

Our conversation was interrupted by the arrival of Joshua, who turned out to be the husband of Mrs Doggett and with him, the newly promoted sergeant Street whom I had first encountered two years previously. Both expressed the same shock and horror on seeing the body as we had.

"What have we here, gentlemen? A heart attack would you say?" asked the sergeant.

"It's possible that we may have a murder on our hands, Sergeant. A swift acting poison may well be responsible for the agonised expression we see on Mr Fane's features and the twisting of his limbs in such a grotesque fashion."

Street turned to me, "Good to see you again Doctor, is Mr Holmes with you?"

"Hullo, Street. It is good to see you too. It is a pity it has to be a sad occasion such as this. No, Mr Holmes has decided against travelling with me on this occasion."

"Oh well, it may be turn out to be a simple case, all the same I would have welcomed his presence here. Tell me, how would he have died, curled up as we see him now or.......?"

"If our assumption of poisoning is correct then death would have been preceded by convulsions of the most violent sort."

"And yet, it's odd isn't it, that although he is dressed for an evening in, there is a top hat by the side of the body which surely would have been disturbed by any convulsive shakes that he may have suffered," Street said.

I had hardly registered the top hat, lying as though placed for effect, next to the body. The point that Street had made was a pertinent one and brought home to me how efficient an officer he was and how his elevation to sergeant was richly deserved. It also stirred vague memories in me that stubbornly refused to bubble up to the surface of my consciousness. The sergeant told us that he would wire Bridport police station to have Inspector Baddeley sent out, now it was confirmed that the death was indeed suspicious. I had no great confidence in Baddeley's powers, having met the man; finding him most insufferable and lacking entirely in imagination and guile.

"I think that we had best preserve things exactly as they are, gentlemen. How do we determine whether death was owing to poisoning?" asked Street.

"Hopefully it can be detected in the organs of the body. Dr Spurr, the Chief Medical Officer for the town will carry out a post-mortem and the presence of poison will be confirmed or not by a toxicology test." Jacobs replied.

"If it is a quick acting poison as you suggest, Doctor, how do you think it would it have been administered?" Street asked.

"If it was something like strychnine it could be easily given through food or drink. If the dose was sufficiently large, death would follow quickly."

"There is a decanter here on this small table," I said, pointing to a highly polished circular table which held the decanter, plus two glasses which had dregs of liquid in both. "It seems Mr Fane had a recent visitor," I added, after sniffing the remains of the drinks; malt whisky in this case.

"Perhaps it is a case of self-destruction?" opined the sergeant.

"The presence of the two glasses strongly suggests that there were two people in the room and surely it must be rare indeed for a person to take his own life in the presence of another," I rejoined.

Sergeant Street nodded, "I have no doubt you are right, Doctor," and went off in search of Mr and Mrs Doggett to inquire as to who may have called at the house this afternoon.

I, for my part was eager to return to Beatrice as was Jacobs to his family. After a few moments the sergeant returned with the news that there had been a caller to the house shortly before five o' clock. At the sound of the door knocker, Mr Fane had called out to Martha that he would open the door himself. Martha had only a fleeting glimpse of his visitor and described him a slim, short man. She stated that she heard nothing further from Mr Fane and was unable to say when the gentleman caller left.

"I think that Watson and I have outlived our usefulness here. I will contact James Spurr regarding the post-mortem. Will you keep us informed, Sergeant?" Jacobs asked.

"Yes of course I shall, no matter how Inspector Baddeley may feel about it."

Just then we heard a commotion in the hall and Mrs Doggett came running into the study.

"Blood," she cried out, "blood in the hall."

12

We rushed into the hall, now lit, to see a crimson tide of blood dripping from behind a painting of Lyme harbour. Once we had removed the picture, I was dumbfounded to see scrawled the single word, 'Rache'.

"I know this, Watson," cried Jacobs, "I have read it in one of your stories."

"Yes you would have done, it was my introduction into the career of Holmes in March 1881. The violent and shocking death of Enoch Drebber. I wrote up the adventure as 'A Study in Scarlet'."

"But what does it mean, Doctor?" asked the sergeant.

"The word itself is the German for 'revenge'. As to the meaning of its presence here I cannot tell unless our perpetrator is telling us that the slaying of Robert Fane is an act of revenge. Drebber's body, incidentally, also had a top hat lying next to it."

"Heaven only knows what the inspector will make of this," sighed Street.

"That, my friend, we must leave to you to find out. Will you be so kind as to keep us informed of any developments," I said

"Of course, Doctor Watson. Good night to you both."

Jacobs checked on Mrs Doggett before we left and gave her a little something to help calm her nerves and together we left that house of death. I arranged to return to Jacob's house later after resuming my quiet evening with Beatrice. That plan was to be rudely interrupted. Beatrice kindly warmed up the plum pudding I had been forced to relinquish and as I was savouring the prospect of this delicious dessert, a loud knocking echoed through the house. I was never one to give credence to lightning striking twice in the same place, but my belief was sorely tested on this occasion. Nathaniel brought an elderly gentleman into the room. He was adorned with side whiskers which had long since gone out of fashion. His brow was furrowed and his whole face deeply lined. His hair was long and unkempt, his voice gruff almost to the point of being unintelligible.

"You are Doctor Watson, yes?" he barked out.

"Yes, that is correct."

"The same Watson who writes about the Holmes chap?"

"Yes, the same, but I..........."

"I am Sir Reginald Bartelby. Robert Fane was my nephew. I want your Holmes down here; I want him to find his killer."

13

"He is not as you put it, 'my Holmes' and I am not at all sure that my friend would be available to undertake any kind of investigation into this sad affair. I am confident that you can leave the police to deal with this. They are here on the spot and have the resources to handle this case to your satisfaction."

"You may have confidence in the police, sir," he barked, "but I do not. Did I fail to make myself plain to you? Do you have trouble understanding plain English? I need Sherlock Holmes. I demand that you send for him."

"You have made yourself very plain, Sir Reginald. Even so I cannot guarantee that Mr Holmes would agree to act for you."

"I suppose it's a question of money is it? It always comes down to hard cash with those sorts of fellows. Well, I have money, sir, let me assure you," he boasted and promptly threw down on the table a bag of coins.

"There you are; one hundred guineas. Try not to spend it on drink or women before your detective friend arrives. I will be in touch."

I was quite incandescent with rage. What an absolutely insufferable man, yet even then I felt I had to make some kind of allowance for his behaviour; after all, his nephew had just met an excruciatingly painful end. All the same I had a strong inkling that Sir Reginald Bartleby conducted all his affairs in this manner and was scrupulously fair in that he behaved abominably to all and sundry. I pushed the plum pudding away, my appetite having been quite taken away.

"I am sorry, Beatrice."

"Do not worry, John. It will keep for another day."

"Thank you, but I was really apologising for the events of this evening."

"But, John, they were events that were entirely out of your control. There is no need of apologies especially to me; I am just overjoyed to see you."

"Thank you. Your sweetness is only matched by your beauty." I picked up the bag of guineas and turned them over in my hand.

"Now, what shall I do with these beauties?"

"Perhaps Mr Holmes could be enticed to Lyme once more?"

"There are certainly elements to this case which raise it above the commonplace. Indeed, the deliberate referencing of an earlier case

14

of Holmes makes it veritably recherché. Ah," I said, seeing Beatrice's puzzled expression, "let me explain."

Once I explained to Beatrice how the scene of the crime pointed quite deliberately to one of our earlier adventures and she understood how the matter was, she was in complete agreement with the decision that I had reached, namely to wire Holmes in the morning with the details as I had them and then await his decision. In due course that evening I repaired to Dr Jacobs's house, too late to catch the children before their bedtime so the nightly stories I had become accustomed to telling them during my visits would have to wait for another day. My day ended with confused, deranged thoughts of poisoning, top hats and words scrawled in blood.

Oct 12

Is there a doctor in the House? Ha Ha. Is there a Doctor in the ~~House?~~
Town? Yes Yes.
Arm in Arm they Strolled along the Seafront. The Fool did not even
Notice me. He only had eyes for his Beloved. He may not even Know
what my Message meant but There is one Who will Know.

Let the Games commence.

And they have. Fane knows that now. How sweet it was to watch him
die. I never knew that revenge could bring so much Pleasure. ~~I could~~
~~have danced for joy~~ *I danced. I swear I danced as his eyes Pleaded with*
me. Mr Fane Mr Fane in so much pain. Ha ha.

I arranged my piece of Theatre like a true Artist. And now the Stage is
set. What will Be will Be.

The Doctor fooled once more. Bartleby!! I played my part to the Hilt and
the imbecile was taken in. Why that interfering oaf Mr High and Mighty
Sherlock Holmes puts up with the man is Beyond me.

The Euphoria of the day has drained me. ~~Sleep will restore.~~ *A night's rest*
will restore my vigour. Tomorrow there is more Work. Ha. Not Work but
Play.

16

Chapter Three

One of my first actions of the new morning after a rather fitful night's sleep was to send off the wire to Holmes with as much detail as I could muster and find the space for. Having done this, and as Beatrice would be busy with her guests for the first part of the morning, I elected to spend some time at the harbour side and observe the various boats and vessels, their crews plying their trade. I often had the notion that one day, maybe in my years of retirement; I would elect to write a short history of Lyme Regis. For such a small town there was certainly a lot to tell; sieges, storms, invasions and many tragedies. The town seemed to have acquired the knack of being in the forefront of British history and it wore its past on its sleeve for all to see. The town's history is a living history and its residents are proud of their community. From a vantage point on the Cobb I was more than content to observe the minutiae of life that goes on in a busy harbour. I noticed Sergeant Street in conversation with Mr Beviss who managed the bonded warehouse in Cobb hamlet and ambled over to see what the latest news was on the previous evening's tragedy.

"Good morning Doctor, I trust you slept well."

"As well as I was able. Have there been any developments?"

"Not really, no. The answer may lay in one of Mr Fanes's business dealings according to Inspector Baddeley, as his personal life appears to be without blemish or scandal. Although he was retired, his former partner, Henry Madders, is still in practice. The inspector is interviewing him this morning. Oh and Dr Spurr, together with his assistant Miss Chapman, is carrying out the post mortem in an hour's time."

I told the sergeant of my visit from the ill-mannered uncle and his decree that Sherlock Holmes should drop everything he may be working on and dash down to Dorset to be at Bartelby's beck and call.

"Are you sure he said that he was his uncle?"

"Yes I am positive. Why do you ask?"

"Well as far as we can ascertain Robert Fane had no living relatives. Joshua and Martha seem fairly sure of this and as they have spent the best part of twenty years looking after the man, it would be safe to assume that they should know."

"Even so, they may be mistaken. Perhaps Robert Fane had reason to deny them knowledge of his uncle."

"That is possible of course, yet they do seem so very insistent and as I say, they should know."

"I am sure there is an innocent explanation. We certainly have no need of further mysteries, Sergeant."

"That's for sure, Doctor! By the way, while you are down this way please feel free to drop in to see me and the wife. Belinda would be so pleased to see you again and between you and me, she does the best plum pudding in the county; you really have to try it to appreciate it."

"Thank you, that is very kind of you. I would welcome the chance to savour any plum pudding at the moment; I'm beginning to think I will never taste it again! Goodbye for now."

Having replenished my dwindling stocks of Ships tobacco at Beers and Sons in Broad Street, I looked in at the post office, but there was no reply as yet from Holmes. I took the opportunity to ask one or two acquaintances in the town whether they had come across the larger than life Sir Reginald Bartleby, but my inquiries were in vain. Still, I had no doubt that the man would put in an appearance when and *if* Holmes did. And if Holmes elected not to come then Bartleby would waste no time in seeking me out to berate me, not to mention regaining his hundred guineas which he no doubt thought I was busy frittering away on Heaven knows what. I saw a figure I immediately recognised walking up the hill towards me and I could find no convenient doorway to duck into before he was upon me.

"Doctor Watson, I knew of course that you were in town. I must say I saw no need whatsoever for Dr Jacobs to drag you along to the scene of Mr Fane's death yesterday. It was a place and time for those on official business. Violent deaths are not meant for tourists you know."

"Inspector Baddeley, I am sure Dr Jacobs did as he thought was right and proper and asked for my assistance. Surely the mere fact that I was there cannot in any way possibly be a matter for the police."

18

"You have Sherlock Holmes's meddling ways, Doctor, that's what worries me. No disrespect intended. Will Mr Holmes be travelling down to show us poor country policemen how to handle our cases? If he does so, will he be favouring us with his fancies and theories? Not after last time I fancy, that's my theory," he laughed uproariously at his own joke and wished me a good day.

The two years that had elapsed since I had last seen the inspector seemed not to have changed the man. His pinched, acid features and haughty air were just as I remembered. He was and is a thoroughly disagreeable man. On a whim I made my way down Broad Street to the offices of Madders and Fane, Family Solicitors and while it was strictly none of my affair I felt sure I could glean something from a brief discourse with Henry Madders. In this I was to be thwarted for a clerk by the name of Matthew Johnson informed me that Henry Madders had not been to the office today nor were his whereabouts known. I asked Mr Johnson whether he knew of Sir Reginald Bartleby, but drew a vacant, blank stare for my trouble. As I was leaving he called me back and told me that Silas Nanther, the senior clerk, would be in the office the following day. Further, that this Mr Nanther had worked for the partnership for nigh on thirty years and he might well be able to shed some light on the mysterious Bartleby. I returned to Coombe Street where Beatrice was waiting patiently for me. We had arranged to go on a picnic in order to take advantage of the unseasonably warm weather and I had secured a pony and trap which were waiting for me at Hutchings's yard.

"Tell me, my love," seeing the well provisioned basket she had prepared, "is the plum pudding amongst those delights?"

"I am afraid not, John. The air would spoil it in no time at all. It's safely wrapped up in a cool spot in the larder and will bear one more warming up tonight."

I tried my very best to avoid showing any disgruntlement or disappointment I may have been feeling and we set off to collect the trap and from there we rode to Stonebarrow Hill which lay on the eastern side of the delightful village of Charmouth. It was a steep climb, but in this part of the world there was nothing remarkable at all about that. The wind brought a slight chill and dampness with it, but the company and the view banished any such petty thoughts. It was a most agreeable and delightful afternoon. How sad it can often be when the simple pleasures in life are neglected. Everyone needs the time to stand and stare; to reflect.

I was in ample time, when we returned to Lyme to repair to the post office to check for a reply to my wire, but there was still no word from Holmes. I encountered Sergeant Street whilst marching down Sherborne Lane towards Coombe Street. He informed me that the inspector had decided that the fact of Henry Madder's absence from his place of business must surely betray his guilt and had therefore issued a warrant for his arrest, posting a man outside Madder's house in the upper part of Silver Street, whilst awaiting a warrant to enter and search the premises, in case he returned there. There were many things that could be said about the inspector, but you could not argue that he was not industrious!

It was too early for any results to be forthcoming from the toxicology tests so everything was in a state of limbo. Elizabeth Hill, Nathaniel's fiancée was to join us for the evening. They had been courting for some two years now and the depth of Nathaniel's feelings towards her was amply displayed by his risking his life for her in those dark times which had engulfed and affected us all so profoundly. Elizabeth was a sweet girl who endearingly called me, 'Uncle John'. In her short life she had suffered immense tragedies; her mother and father were both taken by an influenza outbreak when she was just fourteen and her cousin Rose who was of a similar age had died in the most extreme and sad circumstances possible. Nevertheless, her disposition was enough to brighten any room, her ways engaging enough to capture any heart. The evening passed off quite delightfully; Beatrice had done us all proud with a meal fit for royalty. To close this repast an aromatic apple pie appeared, but as promised, the remains of the plum pudding for myself.

"That looks very appetising, Uncle John. May I have some?"

"Now, now Elizabeth," said Beatrice, "you know full well that particular treat is for John, behave yourself young lady," she said, laughing.

"Please, if you really want it you may have it. The apple pie will do me just as well." I offered.

"You are sweet, Uncle John, but I was only teasing you."

"Perhaps we should bolt the door, mother. We don't want poor John to be foiled again!"

20

I truly believed then that all the fates of heaven were conspiring against me in some vast machination, for just at that point in the conversation there came once more a knocking at the door. Rather cruelly in my view, this produced peals of laughter all round. This chortling had all but died away when much to my surprise Holmes walked into the room.

"Good evening, Mrs Heidler, it is good to see you again. Hullo to you too, Elizabeth. I trust young Nathaniel here has been looking after you."

"He has indeed, Mr Holmes," she replied.

"Have you a spare room that I may take, Mrs Heidler?"

"As it happens, yes I have."

"Excellent. Now I fear I must take the good doctor away."

"To where, Holmes?"

"In the first instance, only to the parlour. Come, Watson."

I slid my dish of plum pudding towards Elizabeth and barely had time to notice the look of triumph on her face before Holmes had whisked me away to the intimacy of the parlour.

"When did you arrive?" I asked.

"I have been in Lyme upwards of an hour and have spent that time wisely; that is to say I have been listening to the idle gossip and small talk regarding Robert Fane. Local inns are a great source of information if you only know how to go about obtaining it. The Volunteer Arms is practically awash with tittle-tattle. Have you come to any conclusions yourself, Watson?"

"I am confident that the answer lies in Fane's professional life for as far as anyone can tell, his personal life seems entirely spotless. The killer has certainly given us the strongest possible indication that the motive was revenge."

"Ah yes. The melodramatic appearance of 'rache'. I believe that this revenge is twofold, not just aimed at Robert Fane, but my friend at me, or more correctly, us."

"How so?"

"Firstly, the killer went to great pains to point us towards 'A Study in Scarlet', literally so, for the blood was his own. Secondly, there was his ploy to bring me down here. An invitation I could not refuse in the circumstances."

"The ploy being the allusion to one of our earlier adventures?"

21

"That and of course his visit to you in the guise of the wholly fictitious Bartleby."

"How could you possibly know that, Holmes?"

"From having a brief talk with Joshua Doggett no more than fifteen minutes ago."

"Even if Mr Doggett does not know of this uncle of Robert Fane's it does not prove his existence or non-existence."

"Bear with me my friend. The information I gleaned from Mr Doggett was that after enlisting the aid of Dr Jacobs he went straight to the home of Sergeant Street and from there immediately back to Seaview Villa. He spoke to no one else regarding the tragedy which leaves one to beg the question as to how Sir Reginald Bartleby, as he styled himself, could possibly have heard of the murder. Unless of course......

"He was the killer. I was well and truly deceived. If only I had known I could have apprehended him then and there."

"Do not worry, you were not to know. Now, if you make yourself ready, we have work to do."

"What work?"

"I have a spot of housebreaking in mind; in fact it will be the house of Henry Madders."

"You suspect him too?"

"No, Watson; my suspicions are of a different nature and need to be acted on with all possible haste."

"I am not sure whether I can be a party to this, Holmes."

"Come now, you have always played the game and will no doubt continue to do so. If it eases that admirable conscience of yours, I can call on Sergeant Street to accompany us."

"He may be as uneasy as I am about this action of yours."

"There will be no problem. I have already apprised him of my suspicions."

"Very well, I will come with you."

"Good old Watson!"

In spite of my misgivings I found it very hard to deny Holmes anything and I was certainly happier in my mind that Street was to escort us, although heaven knows what kind of trouble that would cause for the sergeant with his officious inspector. Henry Madder's house lay not far off and after the sergeant had a few words with the constable on duty and relieved him of his duty we had free access to the house. Holmes produced his, what you may term a 'burglary kit', a collection that many a felon would have been glad of. I am convinced there is no lock that could have defeated the man.

"It's just as well you have never considered a life of crime," opined Street.

"I am convinced if I had, I would have risen to the top of a very crowded profession," Holmes replied.

Within a minute we were in Madder's house.

"What are we looking for, Holmes?" I asked.

"Henry Madders, Watson or certainly the remains of him."

"You think him dead?"

"I am of that belief, yes."

With the aid of the sergeant's lantern we set about searching the property. The ground floor yielded nothing and we mounted the stairs with, for me, a growing feeling of unease, but tinged with excitement too. In a small room off the landing we found our quarry. He was slumped over a sturdy desk which had papers scattered all over its surface, some of which had been swept to the floor.

"It looks as though there has been a struggle," I said to my two companions.

"Yes there has," said Holmes, "but the struggle was against death itself."

"There is something sticking out of his neck," said the sergeant.

"Do not touch it!" shouted Holmes. "Watson, what does this recall to you?"

"The death of Bartholomew Sholto; the poisoned dart! My God, Holmes what games are being played with us here?"

"There appears to be a piece of paper in the gentleman's hand," said Street as he reached for it. He claimed it from the dead man's grasp. "It says..."

"The sign of the four," I whispered.

"Sergeant, could you go and rouse the inspector? Do not worry you will not have to suffer his wrath for long, my belief is that the chief constable now having been presented with two inexplicable violent deaths in two days will have no option, but to call in Scotland Yard. Who knows, you may even receive a commendation for your forward thinking tonight?"

When we were alone we applied ourselves to a diligent search for any clues that our killer may have inadvertently left at the scene. Holmes pointed out various imprints of feet he found on the carpet, believing them to be quite fresh. Rather curiously the marks were uneven in that some were more heavily indented than others.

"Surely he was not running in a small room such as this?"

"No, Watson, he was pacing up and down as he watched his victim die and occasionally he jumped for joy such was the triumph of his revenge. I imagine the same scene would have been played out at the house of Robert Fane as he watched his victim die in agony."

"We cannot know for sure that he witnessed Fane's death, for surely he would be eager to get out the house as quickly as possible to avoid detection."

"The placement of the top hat tells us he did precisely that as does the scrawled 'rache'. We are dealing with not just a vindictive man, but a sadistic one."

"Have you any idea who he may be?"

"There are many who would wish some kind of revenge on me for their loss of freedom, but I can think of no one at present that would go about it in such a fashion or any indeed that would be at liberty to do so. Our initial researches must be with Madders and Fane; somewhere in the dealings of that company we will find the information we seek."

"You forget, Holmes, you do not have an actual client, only a fictitious one"

"I have his hundred guineas; he is client enough for me!"

We had no option, but to await the arrival of Inspector Baddeley. We did not have to wait long before his grumblings about 'amateurs' and 'insubordinate sergeants' could be heard as he ascended the stairs. His mood had not lightened as he entered the room.

"Mr Holmes, Doctor Watson. I should have the pair of you arrested."

"For what, Inspector? Finding a body that you should have discovered yourself? For displaying initiative, where you have displayed none?" Holmes rejoined.

Baddeley glowered at Holmes. "You have interfered with an official police matter and to cap it all you persuade my sergeant to countermand orders. I will see to it that he is up on a charge and you will be the one to blame for any adverse affect on his career."

"As to the sergeant's career, he will rise to the front rank because he has two qualities that you lack, imagination and sagacity. I will say as much in the wire I intend to send to your chief constable in the morning. Good evening to you, Inspector. We will leave you to discover what you may discover and by the way, Inspector, I fancy you can now cancel the warrant you have out for Henry Madder's arrest. Come, Watson."

"What will our next move be?" I asked Holmes as we walked down the lane.

"Along the lines I have already proposed, that is to say to look very closely at the affairs of Madders and Fane. Of course our powers to do that are limited, but if Scotland Yard is called in, it should make our task easier. There is another reason for the urgency of doing so of course."

"What is that, Holmes?"

"We may discover the involvement of others in whatever business has turned our friend to murder. In short, Watson, I am referring to other potential victims."

"There is one point I am not sure on."

"Just one, Watson?" he asked with raised eyebrows.

"If I had not been at the murder scene, it's entirely possible that the clues left pointing to 'A Study in Scarlet' may have gone unnoticed. Our killer was surely fortunate that I was in the town at all."

"It's obvious is it not that he did know you were here. In a small town such as this he would have got wind of your impending visit through one means or another. Admittedly, you may not have attended the scene of Fane's death, but I suspect our adversary had a trick or two up his sleeve to ensure that the clues would become known to you."

"Then my responsibility is doubled, not only is a crazed madman out there murdering at will according to my written word, but also it seems to me that Robert Fane and Henry Madders might still be alive if I had not come to Lyme."

"Not so, my friend. Fane and Madders had been earmarked out for death and your coming here was from the point of view of our murderer either a happy coincidence or part of a grander scheme. True, it may have given him the idea of linking the killings with previous cases of ours and rekindled thoughts of revenge against us, but rest assured the killings would have taken place without your presence just as much as they actually did with your presence."

Upon our arrival at Beatrice's I had to issue yet another abject apology for my absence. We opened a bottle of wine which quickly became two and spent the remainder of the evening discoursing on music, art, Queen Elizabeth and Holmes's new speciality, the life of bees. How odd it was at the end of the day to find myself leaving the company of Beatrice whilst Holmes remained there. Life was never easy, either in love or war.

Oct 13

I wish I had an Audience to bow before. My talent for the Dramatic knows no Bounds. What a Weak man was Henry Madders. Throwing Himself at my Feet. Weak. Weak. He took longer to die than His friend Fane. More time to Reflect on his Death. More time for me to be in Complete Rapture.

Bravo Mr Madders. Your death throes were Exquisite. I applauded you for the Jubilation you gave to me. The Dance of Death of your own became the Dance of Life for Me.

Oh and Those touches! The Dart. The Note. Welcome to my Theatre. The Admission is free but the show will end All too Soon.

It has Worked. There he Stood in the Street as I watched and him not knowing. The Great Sherlock Holmes ensnared trapped and about to be reeled in. You will dance to this Fine Tune of mine Mr Busybody Detective and when the dancing ends so Will You.

What a Game. What a Game.

And More will Play.

Chapter Four

The next morning brought with it the news that Robert Fane's end had indeed been brought about by the use of strychnine. The cause of Henry Madders's death would take a little more time to determine although Holmes was of the belief that his demise had been caused by a lipophilic alkaloid such as the deadly poison which can be obtained from the *Phyllobates terribilis,* the deadly poison dart frog of South America. I had no doubts that his reasoning would be proved to be entirely sound.

The majority of that day passed off in a perfectly ordinary fashion although Holmes spent a large part of it bemoaning the impasse that we found ourselves subject to. I suggested to Holmes that we could best use our time compiling a list of names of those who may wish revenge on him or us. This idea was waived away with a despairing glance as he believed that our quarry would be better run down through the business papers of Madders and Fane. To do that we had perforce to wait for whomsoever Scotland Yard would send down and whoever that may turn out to be, we were confident that they would enlist our help especially in view of how closely we appeared to be connected to the case. Sergeant Street brought us word that the chief constable had indeed wired Scotland Yard just as Holmes thought he would and had received a reply to the effect that one of the Yard's top men would be despatched to Dorset later in the day. We also learned that, as a mark of respect, Silas Nanther, the senior clerk at Madders and Fane had taken the step of closing the office for the day. We would, therefore, have to wait until the following day in our quest to get a deeper insight into the cause and perpetrator of these heinous crimes. Beatrice and I decided on a stroll after luncheon and we left Holmes still bemoaning his enforced lassitude.

A south-westerly was beginning to make its presence felt and from a distance we could see plumes of waves as they cascaded over the Cobb drenching unsuspecting souls who were strolling beneath its walls. More than once I had cause to marvel at this construction that had protected the town and harbour over the previous six hundred years and yet although functional had an innate beauty all of its own.

We spent a most agreeable hour in perfect contentment, the fresh sea air invading our senses. We had been kindly invited to share an evening meal with Dr Jacobs and his family so after our walk we visited Rendall's the grocers in Broad Street to purchase a bottle of Beaune, taking the time also to pick up essential supplies that Beatrice was in need of. Holmes was still ensconced in the parlour when we returned, listless and restless. However, he was more than happy to come with us that evening, something that Arthur and Cecil in particular would be grateful for as they, even at their tender age, were wholly taken with the notion of being a private detective.

Around half past five that evening we had a further visit from the inestimable Street with a familiar face in tow; Inspector Lestrade!

"Good evening, Mrs Heidler," said Street, "I was hopeful that you may have a room available for our inspector from London."

"I do indeed as Mr Willis left today, shall I take your bag, inspector?"

"Thank you, Mrs Heidler, a pleasure to meet you, the good doctor here has spoken of you many times. Good evening Mr Holmes, Dr Watson, I am told this is a bad business."

"Hullo Lestrade. I was expecting your arrival and yes it is, but we have a social occasion to attend tonight which we are all looking forward to so I am afraid discussion of the matter will have wait until the morning. What say you, Watson, do you think Mrs Jacobs could stretch her fare and hospitality to a waif and stray from our great metropolis?"

"I am sure she could, but to observe the niceties I will walk up and ask her in person."

Jacobs's house was only a short distance away and I was back in no time at all with the good news for Lestrade's stomach that there was indeed enough fare to go round. Holmes had been true to his word in my absence and eager as Lestrade was to gather as many details as he could he had met the brick wall of Holmes's resistance. On the occasion of Holmes's previous visit to Lyme he quickly formed a bond with Jacobs's two sons, Arthur and Cecil. It was a reminder that Holmes still had the ability to surprise me; his attachment to the children was something I could not have foreseen. Perhaps it reminded him of the family life that he once had, not that it was something he had ever seen fit to discuss with me. In view of the way that he and Mycroft have

29

grown up; both very private people with no great ability to socialise, I tended to subscribe his connection with Arthur and Cecil to his longing for the kind of childhood that had been denied him. I fully realised that there would be no confirmation of this theory even I elected to broach the subject with Holmes; he was a complex and in many ways an intensely private man especially in matters pertaining to his family. Even now after seventeen years friendship I could not say with any certainty where he had been brought up, schooled and where he went to university. I accepted this paucity of information as being Holmes's inalienable right to privacy; after all it was a full seven years before he casually informed me that he had an elder brother. It is fair to say there was a curious, secretive streak in the man which led to many dramatic effects, but also left even his closest friend almost entirely in the dark as to what his exact history might be. I was nearer him than anyone else and yet I was always conscious of the gap between.

As soon as we reached the door Arthur and Cecil were upon us with squeals of delight and Holmes hugged both of them in turn. Lestrade was introduced to Jacobs and his wife, Sarah and was made most welcome. The two boys, with Violet in tow, were united in their entreaties.

"Will you play detectives with us?" they asked, "it's our favourite game of all."

"Now, now boys, please allow our visitors to settle down, they are not here to play with you after all," said Sarah.

"Mrs Jacobs, I am sure I speak for both Dr Watson and Inspector Lestrade when I say that we would be happy to play," Holmes interjected.

Sarah laughed, "Inspector Lestrade does not look too sure to me, Mr Holmes."

"Are you a real policeman?" asked Cecil.

"That I am, young man."

"And Mr Holmes solves your cases for you?"

"Well, Mr Holmes has certainly been some help to me on the odd occasion," Lestrade said, shuffling his feet and looking decidedly uncomfortable.

"Why, thank you Lestrade! Now, boys, do you remember the story of the Hound of the Baskervilles, I seem to recall Dr Watson telling you the tale?"

In fact I had recounted the tale to them more than once although at present the tale remains unpublished.

"Yes, yes," they shrieked.

"We will act it out although it will have to be briefly as your mother will be a little bit cross with us if we are not ready to eat soon. Lestrade how is your howl? If sufficiently realistic you may act as our hound."

"Howl, Mr Holmes?" asked the inspector.

"Yes, howl," exclaimed Holmes, clapping him on the shoulder. "Children, do we want our good friend the inspector to be the fearsome hound?"

"Yes, yes," they screamed.

"I cannot hear you!"

"YES, YES!!"

I was most amused to observe the look of bemusement on Lestrade's face as the realisation of what Holmes was asking gradually dawned on him. He looked quizzically at Holmes and the children and then cupped his hands to his mouth and proceeded to utter a howl, which every four legged beast and perhaps also the two legged ones in town must have heard and trembled at.

"Bravo!" said Holmes, "I see you have a natural turn for this."

"He is very frightening," piped up little Violet, determined not to be left out.

"Yes he is," replied Holmes. "Now, has anyone got a fishing net?"

"Yes," said Arthur, "it's quite an old one though."

"Never fear. Run off and get it and you can be Stapleton, the villain."

"Did he fish?" Arthur asked.

"No, Arthur," sneered his younger brother, "don't be silly, he caught butterflies."

To the extent that it may be considered possible to condense an adventure lasting several days into a performance lasting thirty minutes then we must be adjudged to have made a success of it, from the very first appearance of Dr Mortimer with his tale of a gigantic hound to the desperate flight and demise of Jack Stapleton in the great Grimpen Mire. The children loved every minute of it although it was fair to say that it was difficult to tell at times just who were the children and who

31

were the adults such was the almost inexpressibly good time that we had. The arrival of the buffet we were to share enabled the older ones amongst us to get our breath back, chiefly me I fear. The selection of cold meats and pies were most appetising with a variety of vegetables as an accompaniment and a promise from Sarah that there was to be a pudding which Beatrice had informed her I would really enjoy. The conversation ranged over many subjects during the meal, none of which had any bearing on the case. Holmes's ability to detach himself completely at times such as these was to me wholly remarkable. He and Lestrade reminisced about cases they had worked on together; Lestrade having a slightly different remembrance about his part in them compared with that of Holmes.

The remains of the main meal had been cleared away when we heard an almighty crash from the kitchen; Jacobs leapt up from his chair and dashed away into the kitchen. He came back in, shaking his head.

"It is bad news, Watson," he said mournfully.

"Can nothing be salvaged?"

"Sorry, Doctor Watson!" called out Sarah from the kitchen.

"Do not worry yourself, the fates are well and truly conspiring against me it seems."

After further good natured conversation a most pleasant evening came to an end and the following morning would see our work begin in earnest. Holmes assured Lestrade that he would apprise him of all the facts he would be requiring on their return to Beatrice's as Lestrade was determined he was not going to wait until the morning for the details of this 'bad business' as he put it. I went to my bed happy, but with a nagging feeling that I had heard something important tonight and could not shake off the nagging thought that I had missed something.

I had no time to ponder on it for Morpheus was laying in wait for me and the ambush was entirely successful.

Oct 14

I could not have Arranged it better. No I cannot take the Credit but I will take something else!!

Scotland Yard send down Their best Man do they? Ha! The place must be full of Imbeciles for them to Think that Inspector Lestrade fits the Bill. He is a Lackey of Holmes. Nothing more. Nothing less. Not for Much Longer my friends.

Their days are Numbered.

~~Just a little More needs to be done~~ There is a touch More work to be Done. I must keep my Wits. Come to Me Gentlemen.

Be My Guests.

Chapter Five

I wandered down to Coombe Street quite early in the morning for I was breakfasting with Holmes and Lestrade at Beatrice's. I assured Sarah that this was in fact prearranged and was in no way a reflection on the non-appearance of the plum pudding yesterday evening which had taken it into its head to spread itself all over her kitchen floor. They were seated already and after a most welcome embrace from Beatrice I took my place beside them. The breakfast was brought into us by a familiar face, one I had not seen for some two years.

"How are you, Lydia? Do you remember me?" I asked.

"Yes I do. You were the man who did all that thinking by the church, just like me."

"That was me. Do you do a little work here now?"

"Yes, Mrs Heidler uses me for cooking and cleaning and the like when she is busy."

"That must mean some very early starts for you."

"Yes, but my mother is always good enough to call me and she has a *very* loud voice. I don't mind getting up because I enjoy working for Mrs Heidler; she is a very nice lady."

"She is indeed, Lydia."

As we ate we discussed our plan of action, namely to repair to Madders and Fane and set about a thorough search of their documents, files and paperwork for any clue as to who may have held a grudge against them. We were certain that there the answer must lie. That was of course only part of the solution for we were involved also; how, we did not know, but whoever our quarry was, he was hell bent on our destruction too, according to Holmes. Or as he put it, 'Not only are we the hunters, but we are also the hunted.'

When we reached the solicitor's office Silas Nanther and Matthew Johnson were already in attendance. After introductions had been effected all round we applied ourselves to the task in hand. Initially, it was decided quite arbitrarily to limit the search to the previous ten years and if that threw up nothing only then would we continue past that time.

"Tell me Mr Nanther," asked Holmes, "did Mr Madders and Mr Fane have specific areas of expertise that they worked in?"

"Not really, Mr Holmes, they were both family solicitors in the usual sense of the term. They dealt with matters of the home, insurance claims and the like and on occasions, inheritances."

"That sounds as though it may be an area which could bear fruit for us; legacies often stir up heated emotions. Do you recall any problems or issues arising out of an inheritance claim that either of the partners worked on?"

"There are always problems, but none that I can think of which could conceivably result in our present tragedies. Wait though; there were two cases that may be of some help to you. They were both some nine years ago and close together as I recall."

Lestrade and I discarded the dusty bundles which we had been perusing and delved into one of the cabinet drawers in search of cases from 1889. These, once located, were spread out all over the floor.

"Do you remember any names, Mr Nanther?" Holmes asked.

"One involved an unsubstantiated claim to the Twynham estate. The estate was very valuable indeed and the legacy was certainly the largest that the partners had ever been involved with and quite possibly the largest legacy ever seen or heard of in Lyme Regis. The claimant was a woman by the name of Beryl Markham. She had no real claim that Mr Fane could determine and to be honest she was given quite short shrift by the partners. I recall saying that much to them, although it was perhaps not my place to do so."

"Did this woman issue any threats?" I asked.

"No, although one thing did strike me on the occasion of her last call to the office."

"And what was that?"

"She was sporting a black eye and a fair old bruise on her forehead, sir."

"Did she now? Someone was punishing her, a puppet master in the wings no doubt," mused Holmes.

"That seems quite a leap of the imagination, Holmes," I said.

"Do you think so, Watson? Well, you may be right, but already an image becomes to form for me as to what kind of man we are dealing with."

"What man? In our inquiries here all we have heard about so far is a woman, this Beryl Markham. What makes you think there is a connection between her and the killer we seek?"

"I have the paperwork here, Mr Holmes," said Lestrade, "the address given for Mrs Markham is one in Tavistock. It's not much to go on."

"Thank you, but Mr Nanther has more to tell us, do you not?"

"As I was saying there was another inheritance claim that year. It followed around two months after the Markham claim I should say. Both Mr Madders and Mr Fane knew the family involved; a very old and well respected Devon family and there were one or two spurious claims to the title and lands after Sir Charles had died."

"Sir Charles Baskerville perchance?" inquired Holmes.

"Yes sir, the very same."

"And who was making the claim?"

"He went under the name, Rodger Baskerville, claiming descent from another of that name. He could not furnish any documentation to support this claim however, nor was there any corroboration forthcoming even to prove he was who he said he was and the title went to a Henry Baskerville. He was very cut up about it; he fair turned the air blue in here and in the end had to be ejected forcibly into the street by the junior partner, James Broderick."

"Rodger Baskerville! I cried, "Surely, Jack Stapleton cannot be behind this!"

"He cannot be, Doctor. That's a ridiculous notion, he perished in the mire," said Lestrade.

"In as much as the body was never recovered we can at least, I suppose, express some doubt about the fact of his death. If anyone could have survived a flight across that bog it would surely have been Stapleton, his intimacy with the pathways across the mire was well established," Holmes stated.

"The butterfly!"

"The what, Watson?"

"I was walking along the seafront on the afternoon of my arrival here and I was jostled by a complete stranger. Immediately afterwards I found a butterfly in my pocket. It must have been he who had placed it there as he brushed against me. I thought nothing of it; it was just a trifling incident. But, why would he do such a thing?"

"Watson, Watson, how often do I have tell you that the little things may be of the greatest importance. My method is founded on the observation of trifles. Tell me, Mr Nanther where can we find this James Broderick now?"

"He left here some three years ago although I forwarded correspondence to him for some considerable time after that. There has been little need of late for such correspondence except I did have a letter from him a short while ago asking for Mr Madder's address and that of Mr Fane's too to enable him to send Christmas greetings to them."

"To the best of your knowledge had he sent Christmas greetings to them before?

"I do not know, Mr Holmes. He certainly had not asked me for the addresses before. Perhaps he had them and then lost them."

"And, did you in fact release that information to Mr Broderick?"

"Yes, I sent a letter with the addresses as requested after first clearing it with my employers."

"Thank you, but, where? Where did you send it to?"

"I have it here somewhere in my address book," he said, pulling out a loose leaf volume from his desk, "ah yes; The Laurels, Sampford Courtenay, Devon."

"Thank you. Did you do much work yourself on the Baskerville claim?"

"Yes I did, Mr Holmes. In my position as chief clerk, a lot of the day to day work would devolve upon me."

"And Mr Broderick, would he have been intimately involved with this particular legacy?"

"Yes, Mr Holmes."

"Would that be just as true with this vast Lyme Regis legacy, the Twynham legacy?"

"The majority of the meetings with Baskerville and those with Beryl Markham were handled by Mr Broderick. I believe he even met with Mr Baskerville away from the office. I expect that is why he displayed such hesitancy when called upon to eject Baskerville"

"Thank you," said Holmes, "one final question; to who did the Twynham estate, this huge legacy actually go?"

"A Sir Hugh Duncan, a Scotsman you understand," Nanther said in hushed tones, as though no worse fate could befall a man than to be born north of the border, "but a nice enough chap for all that. He still lives in the town."

Just then the postman arrived laden down with what would most likely turn out to be letters of condolence and sympathy.

"Good morning Mr Grinter," said Silas Nanther.

"Special delivery for you, Silas. A gentleman in the street gave it to me just now to deliver to you personally."

Hardly had the words left his mouth before Holmes had rushed past him, flung open the door and dashed out into Broad Street. He came back in a few seconds later, shaking his head and muttering to himself under his breath.

"Is this some kind of joke?" asked Mr Nanther of us as he released the contents of the envelope onto his desk. "It appears merely to contain five orange pips. What does it mean?"

"I do not wish to alarm you unduly, but it means you are in danger. The pips are a message that Watson and I know only too well. Now, quickly man, you need to get away from here. Your safety cannot be guaranteed if you stay."

"But surely, Holmes, Stapleton will not move against him now. He knows we are here and that we would have seen the pips. It would be a foolhardy course of action."

"He has laid down a challenge to us and will see it through, I assure you. It is imperative to remove Mr Nanther from harm's way."

"Perhaps we could use Mr Nanther as a decoy or a trap to ensnare Stapleton, that is if he has no objections," put in Lestrade.

"There have already been two violent deaths," said Holmes, "I don't propose to play games with someone's life. Besides, he has his decoys in us, Lestrade."

Nanther's face was a picture of terror, bewilderment and puzzlement. Two days ago he was secure in his position here; now his employers were dead and his own life was under threat. He was trying to speak in the manner of a hooked fish gasping for air. He collapsed into a chair and I quickly unfastened his collar, urging him to take deep breaths and to remain as calm as he could.

38

"I suppose I could go to my brother's, he is in Salisbury, sir," he gasped falteringly, "although I would much rather stay if it's all the same to you; I am not a man for running away."

"Don't be obtuse, man. Your life is in danger. Accept it and act on it," Holmes cried. "Mr Johnson, could you find Sergeant Street for me or failing that, the young constable whose name momentarily escapes me."

"Legg, Holmes."

"Thank you, Watson. Could you ask that one or the other come here to accompany Mr Nanther to his home, Mr Johnson?"

"Yes of course, sir."

Holmes paced around the room, his eyes shining and features set hard. This was the Holmes I thrilled to see, the sleuth-hound and a righter of wrongs. When in this kind of mood he put me in mind of an avenging angel who no man could withstand. Perversely, he also displayed a cool, nonchalant air which had the effect of making him the last man with whom one would care to take any kind of liberty.

"Mr Nanther, could I trouble you to search your memory once more? You have told us about the black eye and bruising on the face of Beryl Markham, but can you describe her a little more fully to us?"

"She was tall, sir, I remember that much, and very elegant. Her long hair was not quite black, but a very dark brown. Her eyes were almost the same hue and she had a slight accent that I was unable to place."

"I suspect the accent was in fact Costa Rican, for it was from there that she hailed. Beryl Garcia of course, gentlemen," Holmes said, turning to Lestrade and me.

"Then her account to you, of her time in England with Stapleton, was not entirely truthful," I said.

"No, she seems to have been a little economic with the veracity of her statements."

"How do we go about finding Stapleton?" asked Lestrade.

"As to that, it is he who will do the finding. I fear I owe you an apology, Lestrade."

"Why so, Mr Holmes?"

"I requested your presence here in the message that I sent to the chief constable, as you are, I believe, the ablest officer that Scotland

Yard has, but now your presence here will put you in jeopardy too owing to your involvement at the climax of the Baskerville mystery."

"I can see the truth of that, but do not think for one moment that it will deter me from my duty."

"Good man, good man."

"He could take us at any time, we are like sitting ducks at a fairground stall," I mused.

"I am of the opinion that he would have something rather grander planned for us. We will just have to ensure that he does not succeed and that the violence he intends to mete out to us will recoil on him. Truly the schemer is liable to fall into the pit he digs for another. Our immediate concern is for the well-being of Silas Nanther and James Broderick."

"Do you intend to go to Sampford Courtnenay?" asked Lestrade.

"Not unless it becomes strictly necessary. A wire to the police at Okehampton, which I believe is the nearest town, should suffice to afford protection to Mr Broderick."

"It may be the case that we are too late, Holmes."

"That possibility cannot be ruled out of course. The question is; if Mr Broderick is still alive and well, then will Stapleton move against us or against him? If the latter, then we may well yet find ourselves in that historic village."

"I have to confess I have heard the name before, but in what context I cannot tell," I stated.

"Think back to your history lessons at school, Watson. I am well aware how long ago that was, but does the Prayer Book rebellion ring a distant bell?"

"That's it! Sampford Courtenay was where it began."

"And ended," Holmes added.

At that juncture Matthew Johnson returned with a fresh-faced Constable Legg. Holmes explained carefully to the rather cowed young man that he was to escort Silas Nanther to his home and then to stick with him as far as Axminster station.

"Is there a back way out of here?" asked Holmes.

"Yes," replied Johnson, "it leads into one of the ginnels."

"Very well, if you, Legg would care to exit with Mr Nanther now and please be aware that speed is of the essence in getting him away from danger. Goodbye, Mr Nanther if you will be so good as to leave your brother's address with us then we can contact you when the trouble has passed."

Silas Nanther did so, his hand shaking so much that the address was rendered nearly illegible. He rose somewhat unsteadily to his feet and with one last haunted look at us left via the back door. Young Mr Johnson's countenance was very nearly as troubled as his senior colleague's had been.

"What now for me?" he implored.

"How long have you worked here? Holmes asked.

"For two years now," he replied

"Then I can be confident that you are not in any personal danger, but as to the position you have here, then I am very much afraid that it is out of my purview and I can be no comforter to you. My advice would be to carry on with whatever tasks you have on hand and await developments."

"And us, Holmes?" I asked.

"First of all, we must wire Okehampton and have someone there check on James Broderick for us and await a reply. Further, we need to locate Sir Hugh Duncan; in spite of the Stapleton's claim to the Twynham estate being spurious, Stapleton would not be inclined to look kindly upon Sir Hugh."

A familiar face appeared at the window; Inspector Baddeley. He seemed undecided whether to enter the premises, his manner being somewhat hesitant. In he came, however, ignoring Holmes and me and addressing Lestrade,

"Good morning. You must be Inspector Lestrade from the Yard. I am Inspector Baddeley and I have been instructed by my chief constable to bring you up to date with this matter without any *amateur* interference."

"Then I am very much afraid that you have gone to this trouble for nothing for I am already fully abreast of the matter, thanks to Mr Sherlock Holmes."

"Well, as to that, Mr Sherlock Holmes has been wrong before and no doubt will be so again. My advice, if you wish to take it, is to avail yourself of all the facilities the local police can provide rather than the half-baked theories of a dilettante like Mr Holmes."

"Inspector Baddeley," said Lestrade, raising himself up to his not that considerable height, "I have the honour to call Sherlock Holmes

41

and Doctor Watson my friends, a category I fervently believe you would never, ever fall into. Now, if that is quite all, I will wish you a good day."

Baddeley turned on his heel and departed without another word, but with several black looks in our direction.

Holmes let out a low whistle, "There are unexplored possibilities about you, Lestrade. I must confess that in your company I live and learn."

"Thank you, Mr Holmes. Now then, what do we do now?"

"You are very like friend Watson, whose instinct is always to do something energetic.   For the moment though we have little choice, but to be men of inaction. The next move surely lies with Stapleton and we must possess our souls in patience until his next movement becomes apparent.   Meanwhile, we will send our wire and seek out Sir Hugh Duncan in which quest I am sure the good sergeant Street can assist us."

We wished young Johnson a good day which seemed an incongruity given the precarious circumstances he now found himself in and walked out into the autumn sunlight bathing Broad Street. Having duly despatched the wire to Okehampton, we travelled the short way to a small courtyard off Church Street where the police house was to be found. We were the recipients of some good news from Street, at least for Sir Hugh, who was currently away in South Africa on business and consequently safe from all harm, from Stapleton at any rate.   The sergeant was of the opinion that Sir Hugh's Scottish accent was so thick that he had severe doubts that anyone in South Africa would understand him.

Street laughed to himself, "he is as Scottish as you can get before it starts to hurt." Still laughing, he brewed a pot of tea for us which was most welcome in spite of Lestrade's constant grumbling about 'doing something'

"It's all right for you, Mr Holmes and the good doctor; you have no one to answer to, save yourselves, but I have superiors who I have to make account to; the commissioners will not take kindly to their purse strings being stretched to cover my drinking tea and playing with children."

"I have an idea in that direction, Inspector," said Street, "it may be a bit radical, but it may just work; in your reports be sure to make no mention of drinking tea or playing with children."

"Very droll, Sergeant," laughed Lestrade.

We sympathised with Lestrade in that we were all acutely aware that we had no course of action to immediately follow. My fervent hope was that it would not take another death to bring that action about. Sadly though, that was exactly the case.

Oct 15

Getting into the house was child's play. I could hardly contain my Excitement as I waited for the old Fool. I Paced and Paced in that Dreary Hell Hole. A Man who is so unimaginative as to Live in a Blacksmiths Forge must not Expect to Live a Long Useful Life.

The Police Constable was No more Than a Boy. ~~*I have a heart*~~ *See what a Heart I have for I was glad to be able to let the Boy live.*

My only Regret was that I was Unable to create a scene worthy of My Talents but the sound of my Stave as it connected with Nanther's thick empty head was as satisfying a sound as I had heard for many a Long Day.

Sleep will come easily to me tonight.

Why can I not remove this blood from my hands?

Let it stay then. And await its kin.

Chapter Six

Street gave us such information as he possessed about strangers in town and tenants fresh to Lyme. In the summer any such strangers would not stand out amongst the crowds of visitors flocking to the town, but this time of year there was more chance of identifying a recent arrival as the town was not as full as it was in the summer months. We resolved to do a round of the shops and provisioners and ask the relevant questions. We included the local inns although Holmes could not see Stapleton spending his time socialising thus especially as he would have the strongest possible reason for remaining incognito. All the same, we would at least be seen to be doing something. We were on the point of leaving on our errand when a clearly out of breath Constable Legg rushed in.

"Sarge, sarge, he's gone," he cried, with great agitation etched on his face.

"Gone? Silas Nanther?" Holmes barked out.

"Yes, sir. He said he wanted to take his dog for a final walk before leaving her in the care of his neighbour. He was only going into the garden so I could see no harm in it. When he had not returned after a few minutes I went to look for him and found the gate at the end of the garden open. I called, but received no reply so I came straight down to see the sergeant."

"Why, of all the downright stupidity. You were charged with looking after this man, Constable. Well, I tell you if..."

Lestrade got no further before Holmes interjected, "The time for reproaching will come later. Give the man some tea before he faints on us, he is looking rather wretched. Sergeant, if you can show us the way, we will leave young Legg here to recover his wits."

"Of course, Mr Holmes. Silas's garden abuts the land to the west of Lyme, overlooking the Cobb. The house itself is in Ware Lane."

"Let us hope that when we arrive all we find will be a lost dog and not a lost life," I added.

45

It was a full fifteen minutes before we reached the house of Silas Nanther. A small cottage which had once been a blacksmith's forge, Street told us. Nanther had painstakingly converted it to the humble dwelling we espied. The garden was a small, overgrown affair. It stretched only fifty feet or so and culminated in a magnificent privet hedge, surprisingly well kept, with an archway and gate set into it. Beyond the gate was a wide grassy track which led one way back into Lyme and the other towards Seaton through the great fissure known as the Undercliff. We had no way of knowing which way Nanther would have gone, but fortuitously we heard the distinct sound of a dog whimpering away to our right. It was only a short distance we had to cover before we came upon the sad sight of Nanther's dog whimpering by the side of her master's body. It was a dreadful vision. His head had been beaten in by repeated blows of some heavy and blunt weapon. If he had heeded Holmes's words perhaps he would still be alive and on his way to Salisbury.

"I think not," said Holmes, breaking in on my thoughts as he was wont to do, "I think you are in the presence of one of the most absolute fools in Europe. I should have foreseen this. Stapleton correctly gauged our actions as I would have done myself in his place and any attempts to beetle Nanther away were doomed from the start. If I was the ideal reasoner that your chronicles portray me to be, Watson, then I should have allowed for this."

"You acted for the best, Holmes. It was your intention to save this poor fellow and if he had not chosen to take his dog out then he would yet be saved."

"I do not believe that to be the case, Watson. I would imagine that Stapleton had already gained entrance to the cottage and was prepared to lie in wait for as long as it took. Nanther, taking his dog for a walk was a stroke of luck for Stapleton and more especially for constable Legg who may have found his life forfeited if Nanther had remained in the house any longer. By God, Watson, it hurts my pride; it is a petty feeling, but it has become a personal matter now and I will set my hands upon this evil man."

The wheels of officialdom began to turn as they must at times like this. The sad scene quickly became a veritable blur of activity. A photographer was found to take pictures from every angle possible of the dead man *in situ*, undertakers stood in a huddled group awaiting their turn to act. They reminded me forcibly of a pack of vultures waiting to pick a carcass clean although they were only doing their job. Dr Jacobs was Silas Nanther's doctor and was called upon to pronounce death; the actual issuing of the death certificate would only take place after Dr James Spurr and Miss Chapman had performed the unenviable task of yet another post mortem. Holmes was standing a little way back from this scene with a look of intense concentration on his face and an air of immobility.

"This is not like you, Mr Holmes", chided Lestrade, "we are used to seeing you chasing around like a demented bloodhound on the scent of God knows what. Are there no clues to be found here?"

"Ah, dear, Lestrade. I fear I must be an object of huge disappointment to you, but any clues to be found here will be made largely redundant by the fact we know who our man is and almost certainly where he is bound and where he goes we must follow. This man is most careful to leave only the clues that he wants to be found. He is pointing out the way for us and that way leads to Sampford Courtenay and as to that; my belief is that James Broderick is alive, I have a very good reason for thinking so and I will be very surprised if a wire from Okehampton contradicts that opinion."

"It appears that our man has given up on recalling incidents from some of our previous cases, Holmes" I said.

"I think this killing was too hurried. Nevertheless, it does recall to me the murder at the heart of the '*Boscombe Valley Mystery*'"

"Yes, there is something in what you say, Holmes but possibly accidentally so and not by design."

"I grant you that," he replied.

We removed ourselves from that dismal scene and retraced our steps into the centre of Lyme, once more to the post office. There was indeed a message from an Inspector Wilton of the Okehampton police. In short it told us that Broderick was at work in his office and had reluctantly agreed to have two constables stationed with him for the duration.

"I think you'll agree, gentlemen that we have to pay a visit to Mr Broderick as a matter of urgency," said Holmes.

"Can we not have a little lunch first?" complained Lestrade good-humouredly.

47

"There will be time enough for eating later, but for now we will board Grove's excellent, if a little uncomfortable I am told, horse-bus service to Axminster station after picking up an essential item from Mrs Heidler's."

"What is that, Holmes?" I asked.

"You service revolver, my friend."

"Unfortunately, I neglected to bring it with me."

"Fortunately, *I* did not."

I made yet another abject apology to Beatrice for another absence on my part. This and my apology she graciously received showing her, as I already knew her to be; the most understanding of women.

We made it to the Royal Lion for the connection to Axminster with seconds to spare and settled down into the rather less than comfortable seats for the seven mile journey to the station. The hard wood of the somewhat precarious seating sent shock waves through my body and I was more than glad when we arrived shaken, but in one piece at the station. The plush of the carriage seat did much to alleviate my discomfiture. The train chugged along merrily on the scenic journey to Exeter where we changed trains. Although the small country train stopped at Belstone Corner, the halt that served Sampford Courtenay, it was agreed between us that we would go on to Okehampton to consult with Inspector Wilton and to keep Mr Broderick in our sights. Holmes explained to us that he had no wish to interview the man at his work, but rather at home, where we may find him more relaxed and conducive to our line of inquiry. Having first established, upon our arrival in the town, that James Broderick was still safely ensconced in his office with two burly constables outside, no doubt trying to look entirely inconspicuous, we hastened to the White Hart for a much needed luncheon, at least on the part of Lestrade and me.

"Do you think Stapleton is here?" I asked Holmes as we supped our ale.

"I think it not unlikely, Watson. He is our puppet master, pulling our strings and watching us move and dance to his tune. And we have no choice but to go along with things as they are until we get our quarry where *we* want *him*."

Holmes did not care to eat, a trait of his by no means unknown to me. Lestrade and I had both opted for Devon dumplings and so filling were they that I swear I was full well before the last mouthful went down. Ordinarily, I would not have been tempted to eat another course, but when the landlord mentioned his wife's home made plum pudding then my resolve fell away. After a few minutes sitting in delightful anticipation of the gastric delights to come, my expectation became reality when a steaming hot pudding was placed in front of me.

"Mr Holmes, Doctor! There appears to be some commotion across the way," cried Lestrade, half standing to improve his view from the window. We followed his gaze and witnessed the constables outside Mr Broderick's office arguing loudly with a man we assumed to be James Broderick.

"I think that is our man. Time for action, gentlemen," Holmes cried.

"But, Holmes......."

"Action, Watson. Come."

With a rueful shake of the head I followed Holmes and Lestrade out of the inn and across the street. The fracas had died down and the man we had seen in dispute with the constables was now walking sharply away in the direction of the station. Lestrade showed the constable his warrant card with suitable gravitas and they explained that it had been their duty to watch the premises of James Broderick, also to go to the gentleman's home with him and wait to be relieved. This was an arrangement that Mr Broderick had no interest in extending and he had made it clear to them in no uncertain terms that he was not going to be a party to this intolerable intrusion on his privacy; he was going home and going home alone. Lestrade scribbled a note for Inspector Wilton, informing him that the three of us would take over from his berated officers and make our way to The Laurels.

Our man was on the platform when we got to the station; the train having been delayed in its departure from Bodmin. We settled ourselves down in the waiting room, anxiously scanning the assorted passengers for any sign of Stapleton.

"The likelihood is," Holmes whispered, "that if he is intent on continuing his evil deeds here in Devon, then he is liable to be in Sampford Courtenay already."

"If that is so, Holmes, then he will know of our presence as soon as we set foot in the village."

"Indubitably, especially as he has engineered it," Holmes rejoined.

The sound of a whistle and the sight of steam rising over the distant hedgerows told us of the approaching train, puffing manfully up the slight incline which would bring it into Okehampton station. We noted which carriage our man entered and loitered in the corridor for the short journey to Belstone Corner.

"When we disembark we will follow him to his home. It is only a short walk I believe from the station to the village."

"I fear he will know we are shadowing him," said Lestrade.

"Assuming him to be an astute man then I am confident he will, but there is nowhere to go save where he is going."

"I must admit I cannot quite fathom the actions of this fellow. Why, having been told he may be in danger does he then dismiss the constables and strike out for home alone? "

"That is what we must endeavour to find out, Watson."

On leaving the train Broderick glanced at us as though we were of no consequence whatsoever and set off towards the village at a very slow amble. His whole posture was of one supremely easy with himself and we could certainly not see any sign of alertness on his face with regard to possible dangers. He looked for the world as though he was enjoying a perfectly pleasant afternoon stroll. Before ten minutes had elapsed we entered what appeared to be the centre and fulcrum of village life. An ancient inn stood at a crossroads flanked on either side by a blacksmith's forge and a small general provisions store. Broderick turned to the right by the inn and sauntered past some fine looking thatched cottages. Their weather beaten stone walls no doubt aged back to the Prayer book rebellion itself in 1549. The rebellion both began and ended in violent death in this prettiest of villages. If we were not aware of the fact that Broderick was heading for his home under the threat of death, it would have been easy to assume the man was on a walking holiday, delighting in the sights, smells and sounds of the countryside. We continued on, this strange, elongated caravan of ours. Upwards out of the village we climbed in this leisurely fashion until eventually Broderick turned up a narrow lane opposite a very small and isolated church looking quite as rustic as its surroundings. The lane led to a dwelling which, although not in any way substantial, dominated the

50

countryside around it owing to its elevated position. The sign which swung in the wind proclaimed it to be Reddaway Lodge.

"Let's keep our senses alert, gentlemen," said Holmes, slipping my service revolver into my overcoat pocket. "Watson, if our friend Stapleton should put in an appearance, have no compunction about shooting him down. He warrants no mercy from us."

Our knock on the door echoed throughout the house and the sound of muffled footsteps could be heard approaching. There followed a delay of several seconds as though whoever was on the other side of the divide was weighing up the consequences of opening the door to us. However, the door duly opened and at last we were face to face with Mr James Broderick, a thin faced man, gangly, with arms and legs that looked as if they had minds of their own.

"Yes, gentlemen? Is there something I may do for you?"

"My name is Sherlock Holmes and we wish to speak with you regarding your late employers Madders and Fane of Lyme Regis. I believe Inspector Wilton of the Okehampton constabulary has already told you a little of what has occurred?"

"He related to me an incident which cannot possibly have anything whatsoever to do with me and then came up with the strange and completely unfounded suggestion that my life was in danger. I gave his constables short shrift earlier and now I propose to do the same with you. Good day, gentlemen, your business here is concluded."

"Mr Broderick," said Lestrade in his most officious tone, "I am Inspector Lestrade of Scotland Yard and if you do not allow us to enter and conduct an interview with your good self then rest assured you will be facing a charge of wilful obstruction. Do you understand?"

Faced with the implacability of the stern faced inspector and the certain knowledge that his threat was no idle one, Broderick backed down and opened the door wide for us to enter.

He showed us into a cramped yet under stocked library saying he would be with us in a few minutes after he had let his wife know that he had visitors. When he returned to the room he was mopping his brow and seemed very ill at ease; a complete contrast to the nonchalance of his amble here.

"Mr Broderick," started Holmes, "you are of the belief are you not, that the very idea you may be in peril as a result of certain incidents in Lyme Regis is just so much nonsense?"

"Yes, I see no foundation in it at all."

"And yet, you sweat freely, your lips are dry so it behoves the question that if you are not in fear of your life, what are you in fear of?"

"Well," he blustered nervously, "if the celebrated detective, Mr Sherlock Holmes and a Scotland Yard inspector come to my house to tell me that fact then who am I to argue? Is it any wonder then that I appear nervous?"

"Watson, could you pass me your revolver please?"

Broderick's eyes flickered nervously at this move on Holmes's part. Holmes held the revolver in the palm of his hand, inspecting it and then seeming to declare himself quite satisfied, took two steps towards Mr Broderick and clapped the pistol to the side of his head.

"What is this tomfoolery?" cried Broderick, "Inspector, I appeal to you, are you going to stand by while this man threatens me?"

"I don't believe I will, sir. If you will excuse me I will just go and stretch my legs for a short while."

"Where is Stapleton?" asked Holmes coolly.

"I don't know anyone called Stapleton," screamed a terror stricken Broderick.

"Perhaps you know him as Baskerville. But, whatever name you know him under you are his confederate now as you were when you assisted him in the matter of a certain Lyme Regis legacy and the claim to the Baskerville estate."

"I have no idea what you are talking about."

"Don't play games with me. Do not believe for one moment that you are safe from him. You are in danger just as we intimated; this man will stop at nothing to achieve his ends. The fact you acted in concert with him will curry no favour with him. Now, Mr Broderick, if you please, where is he?"

All the fight evaporated from Broderick, he was a beaten man. He sat back in his chair with an air of resignation.

"You must understand, Mr Holmes that I knew nothing of the man's murderous intentions"

"That will be for a magistrate or jury to decide," said Lestrade, "the best thing for you to do now is to tell us all you know."

"Yes, I assisted the man you call Stapleton in his claims. I altered documents and managed to destroy others that may have shown his claim in a bad light, but all to no avail. It was greed pure and simple that drove me to it, I cannot deny. You have to believe me that if I had known that the shedding of blood was involved I would not have even begun to consider his request for help."

"Be that as it may, you can do us and yourself a power of good by simply telling us where we can lay our hands on him," stated Holmes.

A loud crack and the splintering of glass caused us all to jump. In James Broderick's case it would be his last ever action for he lay across his desk, an ugly bullet hole in the back of his head.

Oct 15 Evening

I confess I was nearly apprehended. But Right was on my side. My escape was only to be expected. Holmes and Lestrade two breathless wheezing men. How could they have hoped to run me down? Ha. Fools. Imbeciles.

Broderick the turncoat. He can have no quarrel with me. I paid him well for his Help but he was one of those who Poisoned my life. He was of no great Help to me seven Years Ago and he had long outlived His Usefulness. Surely if he wasn't such a greedy grasping fool than he must have known he would pay for His Wrongdoing with his life.

I do not think I have ever Pulled off a Sweeter Shot. I must exercise Caution for I tarried too Long admiring my Handiwork so that the Detective and His Lackey were almost Upon me before I came to my Senses.

How Close I am now to the Prize.

Hah! Tomorrow is approaching and it will spell anguish for some. Ha! ANGUISH!!!!!!!!!!

How can I sleep knowing the Prize is within Reach? But Sleep I Must.

Chapter Seven

Watson, go to Mrs Broderick," Holmes shouted, gun in hand as he and Lestrade bolted from the room.

I met Mrs Broderick rushing down the hall, being thoroughly alarmed by the shot she was on her way to the library. My face told her all she needed to know and she crumpled where she stood and slid to the floor. I administered brandy and when she started to recover I explained as gently as I could what had happened. She was all for seeing her husband, but I could not allow it considering the horrendous nature of his injury. I had never hardened myself to breaking the news of a loved one's death no matter how many times it had fallen to me to undertake that duty. There was no sign of a servant or maid so leaving Mrs Broderick in the drawing room I went in search of the kitchen and strong tea.

By the time I had brewed the tea and taken it to that sad, but brave lady, Holmes and Lestrade had returned. Holmes's brows were drawn into two hard black lines, while his eyes shone out from beneath them with a steely glitter. His face was bent downward, his shoulders bowed, his lips compressed, and the veins stood out like whipcord in his long, sinewy neck. His nostrils seemed to dilate with a purely animal lust for the chase. I left my charge momentarily to return to the library where Holmes was now sitting at James Broderick's desk.

"He has got away from us, Watson. We chased him down as hard as we could, but he had a cart waiting by the church; on foot we had no chance of overhauling him," said Holmes

"The man is both reckless and cunning in equal measure and so damn close to being in our grasp. Why, it fair makes my blood boil to think of the man and his crimes," said Lestrade bitterly.

"What sense can we make of any of this, what is the object of this never ending cycle of misery, violence and fear?" Holmes asked of no one in particular as he rifled through the drawers in Broderick's desk.

Bundles of correspondence, receipts and various household bills were scattered across the floor, falling like a paper whirlwind.

"Nothing, nothing," cried Holmes despairingly.

"What I fail to understand, Mr Holmes is why, having got the three of us in the same place, Stapleton should leave us unscathed?"

"Whilst it may have been easy for him to take action against us, I do feel he has something else planned for us as I have stated before and tonight, as well as spelling death for Mr Broderick, is part of this cat and mouse game he wishes to play with us. His twisted mind demands nothing less," Holmes replied.

"I must return to Mrs Broderick and see if there is a neighbour who I can ask to come and keep her company."

"And I must start the official wheels turning. God only knows what my colleagues at the Yard would make of this; sent to Dorset to investigate two murders, only to have two more committed, one under my very nose."

"Be of good cheer, Lestrade," said my friend, "they will think only highly of you when you have captured your man."

Mrs Broderick was able to pinpoint a kindly neighbour for me, a Mrs Austin, who lived in a house which stood just a few yards from that isolated church. There was an embroidered sign above the door which proclaimed the merits of performing a random act of kindness a day. The door was ajar and I shouted out Mrs Austin's name. She answered me and asked me to come straight in. I found her hard at work on an exquisite looking water-colour. She explained she was a writer and illustrator of children's books and was currently working on the tale of Melody the doll that had lost her singing voice. Busy as she undoubtedly was, she dropped everything and came back with me and gathered Mrs Broderick under her wing.

Lestrade in the meantime had gone to the station and telegraphed to Inspector Wilton. We were awaiting his presence and the whole entourage that would follow in his wake. Holmes's searches had revealed nothing.

"Where is he, Watson? Is his work done here? Has he gone back to Dorset? How and when does he intend to strike against us?"

"Perhaps there are others that he perceives as having opposed his interests, who may have played their part in the Golding legacy or the Baskerville claim?"

"Undoubtedly that is a distinct possibility, but unfortunately we are completely in the dark as to who they may be, if indeed they exist."

It was a full hour before the inspector and his colleagues arrived from Okehampton. Our recital of the pertinent facts as we knew them did not occupy too much time and the inspector, perhaps rather surprisingly, had very few questions for us; perhaps the result of being in awe of both a Scotland Yard inspector and Mr Sherlock Holmes. Holmes scribbled in pencil on a piece of paper, folded it and handed it to the inspector.

"Some little pointers for the inspector and an instruction or two," Holmes said, enigmatically. "As we have outlived our usefulness here, I think a return to Lyme is in order." He looked down at the body of James Broderick.

"Why, my friends? Why do people put their trust and their lives in those who least deserve it? How can greed bring a man to this?" he said, shaking his head.

The vagaries of the Mid-Devon train timetable and the unpredictability of their engines ensured that our trip to Lyme was anything, but smooth. We had wired ahead for William Curtis, whom Holmes and I had met before, to meet us at Axminster station with his dog-cart and as things transpired he had to wait upwards of an hour for us. During the seven mile journey to Lyme Regis, Mr Curtis let us know in very minute detail exactly how he felt about having his time wasted, repeatedly so in fact!

We could form no plan for the morrow other than the interrupted errand of searching out strangers in Lyme who may have arrived or been noticed over the preceding days and weeks. Lestrade cajoled Holmes into accompanying him to an inn, 'any inn,' as the inspector put it. The inn of choice turned out to be the Volunteer Arms at the top of Broad Street, where the blazing fire would keep at bay the chill of an October evening. As tempting as this sounded, I was more than happy to let them to go as it meant I would have the evening to myself and therefore Beatrice too, acutely aware as I was that I had seen so very little of my beloved during the last two days. She is the most understanding of women and there was no hint whatsoever of admonishment in her voice for my recent abstraction from her company. We discoursed long into the evening before I bade her good night and set off reluctantly for Dr Jacobs's abode.

Oct 16

Time for Reflection amidst this Joy. When I am Master. What Then? When my Triumph is Complete What Then?

My Contentment will know no bounds.

~~I will have only what~~ ~~My possession will~~ To the victor go the spoils. I am
      the Victor and ~~The Spoils~~
Those spoils belong to Me.

People Will ride by. Point me out to their Children. There he is little ones Lord of the Manor. Joy unconfined. Exultation with No End.

The Stage is Set. I Await my Reluctant Players.

What a Game. What a Game.

But everyone will lose ~~bar me~~ but me!!!

Chapter Eight

Mindful that I was also neglecting my hosts as well as Beatrice, I partook of a leisurely breakfast with Jacobs and his family. Arthur and Cecil were looking particularly handsome in their pristine school uniforms and were positively eager to get to school, which was a far cry from my own feelings about education at their age. Eager as they were to be leaving for school, the entirely expected request to relate another adventure to them duly came. I promised that I would do so at the very next opportunity. By the time I was ready to leave there, having washed the dishes as a kind of penance, Jacobs's first patients were just filtering into his waiting room, so long had I tarried.

Holmes was deep in thought in the parlour at Beatrice's, his cherrywood pipe clenched between his fingers.

"There is coffee in the pot still, Watson, but be so good as to save some for Lestrade, I feel he may well be in need of it."

"Have you eaten, Holmes?" I asked, ever mindful of his habit to go without food when in the middle of a case, sometimes for days on end.

"Yes, thank you. Young Lydia was here again and prepared a magnificent breakfast although I did not then have to wash up afterwards to pay for it as you evidently did."

"My cuffs?"

"Yes, your cuffs."

"Are we ready to go on our mission, Holmes?"

"I certainly am, but as for friend Lestrade I suspect not; he has not risen yet."

This was in fact the cue for the inspector to make his rather unsteady entrance, grabbing the door frame for support.

"I have, but only in a manner of speaking, Mr Holmes. Oh, my poor head," he groaned as he slumped down in a chair, holding his hands to his head.

"Here," I said, handing him my coffee, "I believe your need is greater than mine."

"Thank you, Doctor. I swear I will never drink the merest drop of cider again as long as I live. My insides feel as though they have been kicked by a mule with iron-covered hooves and there appears to be a man in my head, an extremely burly man I shouldn't wonder, who is intent on beating the inside of my skull with a hammer."

The copious amounts of coffee we made him drink had the effect of restoring a little bit of vigour to the inspector and the face cloth soaked in cold water which Beatrice had applied to his forehead had caused the man with the hammer to cease his erstwhile beating activity.

We had decided to start making our inquiries into strangers and the like, in the Cobb hamlet area where the proximity to the sea hastened Lestrade's recovery a little more, but only a little! We received all manner of descriptions of strangers from the short to the tall, the mysterious to the suspicious, the shabby to those in their finery, but nothing that acted as a firm lead that could be followed up in a worthwhile fashion. The area by the Cobb by virtue of being Lyme's harbour was of course more than likely to have a greater share of visitors than the town itself. The proprietor of Rendall's in Broad Street told us of a newcomer to the town who had been in for provisions. He was a slim, shortish man who was not forthcoming about where he was from or where he was living.

"He pays in cash," Mr Rendall said, "and refused all notion of having his groceries delivered."

"Thank you anyway, Mr Rendall. It is a great pity we do not know where precisely to find him, but it can't be helped."

"Well, gentlemen, I may yet be able to help you with that."

"Go on," said Holmes.

"My lad, Leon, saw him coming out of a house in the upper part of Haye Lane. I don't know if he recognised Leon, but he says he pulled his hat down over his face a bit sharpish like. Here's Leon now, he can tell you himself. Could you tell these gentlemen about the chap in Haye Lane, you know, the secretive one?"

Leon entered the shop from a back room, his forehead glistening with sweat and his hands grimy. Whatever else he was, he certainly appeared to be a hard worker.

"He didn't want to be seen I know that much. I was bending down on account of having dropped my bag of butterscotch all over the road." He demonstrated what he meant by pulling out a bag of butterscotch from his pocket and promptly dropped them all over the shop floor where they rolled in different directions.

The three of us found ourselves on our hands and knees attempting the recovery of Leon's sweets. We deposited as many as we could gather into his sticky bag. I saw fit to warn him about the dangers of eating the now contaminated sweets.

"Bit of dust won't hurt, sir. Tastes better for it I reckon."

"Now, Leon," said Holmes, "tell us what you saw."

"Like I say, I was picking up my sweets and saw him coming out of a house," he said, putting his hand once more into his pocket.

"No more demonstrations please, Leon," Holmes said, wiping the dust from his trouser knees, "just tell us what you saw."

"Well, I don't think he wanted to be seen because when he noticed me he pushed his hat down so hard it must have taken him ages to get it off. I saw another man there too, another day that was though."

"That is interesting, Leon. Can you describe him for us?" Holmes asked.

"You'll think me strange, sir."

"Why would I do that?"

"Well, the gentleman had straggly grey hair and side whiskers and looked very old, as old as Mr Rendall even."

"I'm sure the gentlemen are not interested in your opinions, Leon," said Mr Rendall.

"On the contrary, I assure you we are very much in favour of hearing Leon's opinions. Do go on, why would we think you strange?"

"You see, sir although he looked to be an elderly gentleman, it was the same man, he didn't fool me."

Inwardly I groaned. He had certainly fooled me.

"Thank you, Leon," said Holmes and then to me, "there is your Bartleby, Watson, not that we were in any doubt of course. Has this house got a name?"

"It's called Laburnum Cottage."

"Thank you and thank you for your time and yours too, Mr Rendall."

"Glad to have been of some help to you, is there anything else I can assist you with?"

"Yes, Mr Rendall. Have you anything you can recommend for clearing a slight headache?" asked Lestrade.

"Have you been overdoing things?" laughed Mr Rendall, "my advice is to pop up to George Henley; he owns the chemist's just a little way up the street. I am sure he can put you on the road to recovery, sir."

"Alas, Lestrade," said Holmes as we left the shop, "you have brought this upon yourself and you will have to worry about your self-inflicted pain later. I believe we need three things: the good sergeant Street, young Legg and a revolver and then we can declare ourselves ready to pay a visit to Laburnum Cottage."

"Stapleton seems to be engineering and therefore predicting our movements so will he not be expecting such a move?" I asked.

"I think not, Watson. Our finding his dwelling was fortuitous indeed and I doubt he would have foreseen it so we will grasp the opportunity afforded us forthwith."

It took some little time to assemble our raiding party, but in due course we were on our way, ascending Haye Lane. Laburnum Cottage was a modest enough dwelling, a little uncared for maybe, but certainly not in any way neglected. I stayed by the front door with Legg and Street whilst Holmes and Lestrade made their way to the rear to affect a break in with the minimum of fuss. I had my revolver in my pocket which gave me a little comfort, but not much in the way of confidence. The sound of glass and wood splintering carried on the breeze and as the front door began to open I released the safety catch on my revolver and steeled myself for whatever was about to happen. I was relieved to see Holmes's face peering out at us.

"The bird has flown," he announced.

Inside, there were signs of recent habitation for all to see, but a more thorough search suggested that it was unlikely that Stapleton would return, there being no clothes or food. The writing desk which stood prominently and rather oddly in the hall had a few scraps of paper strewn over its surface. Conspicuous on these were the names of Madders, Fane, and Nanther with symbols marked next to them and also our names; save for Street and Legg.

"The house has been available to rent since the end of the summer," said the sergeant, "perhaps the letting agent has some intelligence on where we can find his latest tenant?"

62

"I think it unlikely that our quarry would have left anything that will lead us to him before he *wants* us led to him," Holmes opined. "We have no recourse but to play the waiting game."

The sergeant made his way to the letting agent to report the accidental damage to the back door of Laburnum Cottage that his constable had discovered whilst on his beat. Lestrade had a report to compose and send back to the Yard and professed no idea what or what not to say about his apparent lack of progress. The *Western Morning News* devoted many pages to the grisly murders that had shattered the peace of this small town, speculation was rife, much of it ill-informed, about the causes and where the supposed madman would strike next. To add to the inspector's woes their chief reporter was hoping to track him down for an exclusive interview. Sherlock Holmes was mentioned only as a footnote to the main story:

'Inspector Lestrade, it appears, has enlisted the aid of the amateur detective, Mr Sherlock Holmes who is currently in Lyme Regis on some business unconnected with this series of murders. The view of this paper is that the official police are the best ones to pursue this hunt and there is no need for the interference of amateurs'.

Holmes had the briefest of glances at the leader before stepping into the post office. He came out seconds later with a cable in his hand.

"From Wilton, I asked him to check on a few things for me."

"So I understood. What has he to report?" I asked.

"Briefly, I asked him to ascertain who was in residence at Baskerville Hall, Lafter Hall and Merripit House. He has enlisted the aid of a special constable that is used in such wildernesses; usually a reliable, honest man who can supplement his income a fraction by acting as an unofficial police officer, albeit with official backing."

"You expect that Stapleton would have gone to ground in familiar territory?"

"It is certainly one train of reasoning and there are very good grounds for thinking it to be the correct one. What better location for him to take sweet revenge than the one where we originally thwarted him?"

"Does the report bear out that hypothesis?"

"There is a full report to come by post which should reach us by tomorrow at the latest. Initially, though, it seems that all is as it should be."

"I seem to recall that Sir Henry was none too enamoured of life among the poor folk of the moor and elected to return to his farming life in Canada."

"You recall correctly, he returned to Canada a considerably richer man of course. Baskerville Hall is due to be turned into a private school and a caretaker, a Mr Glanvill and his family maintain the building and grounds in the meantime. Do not let me keep you, my friend if you are eager to spend some time with Mrs Heidler. There is little we can do for the moment and I am quite happy to be left to my own devices."

"If you are sure, Holmes?"

"I am, Watson. I will see you a little later."

Lestrade was sitting in the parlour with a blank piece of paper in front of him, looking as disconsolate as I had ever seen him.

"I don't know where to start, Doctor and that's a fact," he complained.

"Leave it for a day, you may find you have something positive to add to it then."

"I hope so, I truly hope so."

The news we received on the following day in the shape of a letter from Inspector Wilton at first seemed to offer no advance. The news from his special constable was that having inspected all the properties that Holmes showed an interest in, he had to report that all was well and the tenants were who they should be and none appeared to be under any duress. The inspector affixed the constable's report to his own missive and we duly noted his name-*Bartleby*.

"So, he makes his move," declared Holmes, "and Baskerville Hall is once again to be our destination."

"Why not Merripit House for instance, Holmes, it was the chap's home for a short while."

"Yes, Watson, but his ultimate prize was Baskerville Hall and that's where he awaits us. Are we game, gentlemen?"

We gave our assent to Holmes immediately. This man would pay for his heinous crimes and if we could bring that about then we would be only too pleased to do so. It was decided to travel down to Devon the following morning giving ourselves time to prepare both physically and mentally for what lay ahead.

"Should we wire Wilton and have his men keep an eye on the hall in case he flees in the meantime?" asked Lestrade.

"Perhaps, my friend you have not grasped the situation correctly. He will not flee; he has us, his flies, speeding towards his web. Well, he will find his own tangled web will ensnare and trap *him* on this occasion."

Beatrice was spending the greater part of the morning at the home of Mrs Irene Hannington, who was Elizabeth's aunt, discussing and acquainting themselves with the latest fashions in needlework. She left shortly after breakfast had been served in order to be back in good time to take part in a charity lunch for fallen heroes. The lunch had been organised by the local Women's Guild and was to take place in the Assembly Rooms which was located a fair distance from Mrs Hannington's residence which was closer to Uplyme than Lyme Regis.

I had taken up a kindly invitation by Street and his good lady, Belinda, to join them for a simple lunch. Belinda proved to be an admirable hostess and the lunch although simple fare was palatable in the extreme. What made it even more of a delight for me was the sudden appearance of a rich looking plum pudding which was positively crying out to be devoured. The spoon was in my hand when I heard Nathaniel's voice and he burst into the room in a state of extreme agitation.

"Doctor, doctor," he cried, unable to get any other words out.

"Calm down, Nathaniel. Sit down, take some deep breaths and tell me what has happened."

"It's mother, she set off for Mrs Hannington's this morning, but Elizabeth has come to me just now saying she has not been to the house at all and her aunt has not seen her for days. Elizabeth also..........."

"There may be an innocent explanation," I interrupted," perhaps she realised there was more work to do for the lunch than she had anticipated and has gone straight to the Assembly Rooms."

"But, Doctor, Elizabeth has mother's needlework bag. She found it on the side of the road near The Black Dog. How came it to be left there? What can have happened to her?"

Only then did the full enormity of the situation hit me. My stomach lurched and I felt cold and hollow, my heart hammering. I knew in an instant that this could only be the work of one man. The realisation that my involvement with the Stapleton affair had placed Beatrice in grave peril was almost too much to bear. I prayed as I had never prayed before, that she would be found alive.

65

Oct 16 Evening

Easy. So easy.

Their pets are with me now. And I have my own pets too. And soon they will come too. Careering into my Web like the insignificant flies they are. But the spider is not Me. Oh no. Ha ha.

Mycroft Holmes. Beatrice Heidler. My aces in the hole. Here with me now.

What a poor excuse for a man is this Mycroft. Grotesquely fat. No man of Action or Thought is He. Unsuspecting and Gullible.

At least the idiot doctor's woman had the Decency to put up a Struggle. Which Thrilled me though her Resistance was in Vain. Perhaps she would have struggled more had she known what Part she will Take in Tomorrow's games.

Love. Death. The two will Meet on the Morrow.

There will be only one Winner. Death.

Chapter Nine

"I can have every available able-bodied man in Lyme out looking for her, Doctor and they would be glad to do it for she is very well respected in the town."

"Thank you, Street," I said, desperately trying to remain calm and in control of my emotions, "but I fear she is many miles away by now and I know precisely who has her."

"Who? Who has her? What can we do?" asked Nathaniel.

"Come Nathaniel, I will walk home with you," I said, "and you must trust Holmes and me to bring your mother back to you. Look after Elizabeth as you have always done."

"Whoever has her, I am not afraid of them," he stated.

"No one doubts your bravery, Nathaniel, least of all me, but please do as I ask and have faith and trust. I promise you that I will not let anything happen to your mother while there is breath in this body of mine."

We left the police house and walked back down to Coombe Street together. I was entertaining the fruitless notion that when we arrived we would find Beatrice there, suitably apologetic for having alarmed us so. It was futile, I know, but these are the thoughts that one clings to when the reality can be too hard to bear. Not only did I have to bear it I also had to take steps to bring normality back to our lives. Holmes was in the hallway in the process of putting his overcoat on.

"My dear fellow, I was just coming to find you. I am so sorry that this should have happened, however, we know where she is or at least where she is bound. Obviously, Stapleton has taken steps that will absolutely guarantee our presence at Baskerville Hall."

"Instead of talking about it, Holmes, can we not just set off in pursuit now? The woman I love is in the gravest of danger and it woe betides me to discuss it further when we could be doing something."

"She is safe and will remain so and our best chance to effect a rescue is by day not by night which it certainly would be by the time we arrived at Baskerville Hall."

"She may well be safe, Holmes, but she will be isolated and alone. She will be scared. I cannot bear to think of her in that man's clutches."

"I know, my friend. I know," said Holmes gently.

A knock on the door sent both Nathaniel and me sprinting down the hall, convinced this must be news of Beatrice. It was a telegram boy with a wire for Holmes.

"Well, well," said he as he read it through, "the plot thickens."

"Who is it from?"

"Mrs Hudson, the last person I would expect to hear from in this fashion. It seems we have had a couple of gentleman callers to our rooms, looking for brother Mycroft."

"He can hardly be the most difficult man to find, surely:"

"It seems he is at present, for he has not been seen at his office for the past two days."

"Perhaps he wanted a holiday, some men do you know."

"Nay, not Mycroft. His life runs on rails; his lodgings in Pall Mall, Whitehall and the Diogenes Club; they are the rails he runs on. To find him deviating from these except in the direst emergency would be akin to a planet leaving its orbit."

"You think Stapleton has him too?"

"I think it entirely likely. Mycroft could possibly be enticed away if he was convinced that his younger brother were to be in deadly peril; an urgent telegram along those lines might just have the effect of forcing Mycroft to abandon his routine."

"What need has Stapleton of Beatrice or Mycroft? He knows that we will confront him, indeed as you say he has engineered it so I cannot see what he hopes to achieve by holding them hostage."

"I fear that will become clear to us, Watson. Do not worry," he said, laying his hand on my shoulder, "we will recover our loved ones and bring Stapleton to book, before one court or another."

I cannot now recall in detail how we spent the rest of that day although I do recollect that only Lestrade had any inclination to eat. He prepared himself a meal and inviting as the aroma was, my appetite was non-existent. The conversation was stilted and uneasy between us, each of us lost in our own private thoughts. Holmes sat immobile in one of the parlour chairs, his knees drawn up almost to his hawk-like nose, smoking pipe after pipe. The clock on the sideboard chimed to proclaim another hour had gone by; was the time going too slowly or too quickly? My brain had been thrown into disarray by the day's events and the passage of time meant very little to me other than it brought me closer to Beatrice. The realisation dawned on me that I would do anything, absolutely anything to save her.

I elected to stay at Beatrice's that night rather than inflict my misery on Jacobs and his family. I retired with no thought of sleep, but sleep came and with it a strange, fantastic dream. In my dream I was approaching Baskerville Hall, its narrow, high towers visible over the trees, but these towers were hundreds of feet high and they were covered with a host of demons crawling towards the apex of each tower. Their faces were hideous, their lips drawn back in evil grins revealing rows of pointed, blackened teeth. Each of them had an arm extended, dragging a figure with them as they ascended; and in each case the figure was the same; Beatrice. Thousands upon thousands of demonic monsters dragging thousands of Beatrices with them. I tried to cry out, but I was hoarse with fear. Then, seemingly to an invisible command, all the demons released their precious cargo and many thousands of Beatrices fell tumbling to the ground and yet when each one reached the earth, the solid soil turned to the swamp of the great Grimpen Mire and each one was sucked down into that foul morass. I woke with a start, the bedclothes wringing wet with my sweat which was still pouring off me. It was light outside, yet all was silent as the grave. I shuddered and attended to my toilet.

There was an impenetrable thick, blue fog downstairs. I threw open a window and the door for much needed air. Holmes was where I had left him, not that I found this in any way surprising.

"Have you not slept at all, Holmes?"

"There will be time enough for sleeping later when our work is done."

"I only hope that we can bring this man's life of crime to an end."

"Remember, Watson, we have faced greater evils and come through. We will add Stapleton to our Baker Street collection before this day is out."

Lestrade was a little tardy rising, but was fully prepared for our day's work yet was still of the opinion that we should let Inspector

Wilton and whatever body of men he could muster congregate on Baskerville Hall.

"I cannot permit it, Lestrade. One false move, however well meaning from an officer, could prove fatal to my brother and Mrs Heidler. Stapleton is already deranged enough without provoking him to further rash actions."

"As you wish, Mr Holmes. I do feel I have no choice, but to run with you on this one."

"Now, we are deplorably short on weaponry. Watson's revolver is an excellent argument in most situations and I do have a certain little something up my sleeve. Remember, we have not the element of surprise on our side, in fact we are expected in the manner of house guests, but when the time comes for all or one of us to act, act we must."

Nathaniel served us coffee before we set off. He was looking most abject and seemed close to breaking point. I reassured him that all would be well and we would be back before nightfall with his mother. How easy it appeared to me to be able to instil confidence in someone else when you had so very little yourself. Nevertheless, lack of confidence notwithstanding, I was determined to see it through, nothing on earth would deter me.

The bleakness of our mood was matched by the damp, dismal conditions which greeted us. The rain was steady and unremitting, the ride to Axminster in the horse-bus a cold, biting one and the ensuing train journey did nothing to warm or cheer us. We supped warming teas whilst we waited at Exeter station for the country service that would take us into the very heart of Dartmoor. It seemed like an eternity before our train duly pulled into the station. The journey was a swift one, the green squares of fields giving way to a more basic landscape, harsh and unyielding. I caught sight of a grey, melancholy hill in the distance, its jagged summit rising up into the cloudy sky and realised we were very nearly at journey's end.

The train pulled up at a small wayside station and we all descended. Outside the station by a low, white fence there was a wagonette waiting. The driver called out to us as we were preparing to make our way on foot, "Would you be the party for Baskerville Hall?" and invited us aboard.

In a few minutes we were flying swiftly down the road. Cottages here and there lay half hidden in the woods and spinneys which dotted the side of the road, but in the gaps we could see the long curve of the moor with jagged hills standing as sentries. The road, once broad now narrowed to a track and seemed to be swallowed whole by the crags which rose above it. The rain eased and the mist cleared to enable us to look down into a cuplike depression in which stunted trees told of nature's fury which had never been wholly tamed here. Over the trees we could see two high, narrow towers standing out against the sky.

Baskerville Hall. The scene of my nightmare.

Oct 17

Baskerville Hall is mine. I will never give it up.

I have sent that simpleton of a coachman to collect my Guests. They are on their way but their destination will be the Grave but not before we have played a game or two.

They will Watch but they will have no time to Learn.

My pets, such pets as can bestow life or death, are ready to play.

My hour Approaches. The clock is ticking matching my beating heart. Joy. ~~Uter~~ Utter Joy like I have never Known. Long have I ~~thu~~ thought about this moment. Long have I ~~imgin~~ imagined it. My hand ~~shke~~ shakes so much I can scarcely Write.

I hear hooves. A carriage.

Welcome to Your Death Gentlemen!!!!!!!!!

Chapter Ten

The driver spurred the horses on through a track whose ruts were knee deep in leaves. The wagonette slithered and slid, but remained on course. A short while after our first sight of the hall we arrived at the lodge gates, their intricate tracery blazoning the power and wealth of successive generations of Baskervilles. The pillars on which the gates hung were topped with the boars' heads of the family crest.

We sped on through the avenue to a vast expanse of turf which formed a semi-circle around the front of the house. All the Baskervilles through the centuries had left their mark on this, their family seat. Each had added to the showcasing of their wealth. From a huge central block there rose the two towers, ancient and crenellated and now overgrown with ivy that blocked up its loopholes in nature's revenge.

There were a few lights burning to alleviate the house from the gloom of the day and just a single plume of smoke escaped from one of the hall's ancient, twisted chimneys. We stepped down from the wagonette and before our feet had hardly reached the gravel, the driver spun it around and was going hell for leather down that great avenue.

"This is it then, gentlemen," said Holmes in hushed tones, "do nothing foolhardy, but wait until the opportunity presents itself to turn the tables on this lost soul."

A dull, yellow light shone through the heavy, mullioned windows on either side of the door. This slight gleam escaped from under the door and formed a thin ribbon of light in the porch as if it were a line we dare not cross. We could discern no movement from within and Lestrade broke the silence with an act of bravado which endeared the man to me.

"Are we going to stand here all day? Or shall we just walk in? We are expected are we not?" and with that, he pushed against the heavy, oak door which opened noiselessly and we tentatively entered the hall.

It was as I remembered it; large, lofty with coats of arms and medieval weapons adorning its walls. The light was subdued and dim, but we could clearly see the figure of Jack Stapleton standing at the end of this vast hall, levelling a revolver at us.

"Good evening, gentlemen," he said as he approached us, "you will excuse me taking liberties I am sure," as he deftly searched us for weapons. My revolver was taken and thrown onto an ottoman.

"Now," he continued, "no rash moves please. The door to your right leads into the dining room, but of course you would know that. There is a warming fire and oh yes, we have other guests whom you will recognise."

We marched into the dining room which I remembered as a place of shadows and gloom and the atmosphere that night served to heighten that feeling. In front of the cavernous fireplace were two chairs upon which were sitting Mycroft Holmes and Beatrice, bound securely to their seats.

"Beatrice," I cried, "are you harmed?"

"Doctor Watson, you will not speak to my guests without my permission, do you understand?"

I clenched my fists and was looking for ways to act against this devil, but a look from Holmes cautioned me against anything rash.

"Doctor Watson, you will find a coil of rope behind you, please pick it up. Mr Holmes, if you would be so kind as to sit in the vacant chair opposite your brother. Yes, that's it, thank you. Doctor, please bind your friend to the chair and then his wrists together. Do not attempt any chicanery; I will test your handiwork shortly."

I had no choice, but to comply. Holmes had a detached air about him, a coolness of manner which intimated everything was under control. I bound Holmes to the chair as directed and his wrists as he offered them up to me. Stapleton pulled on the rope and satisfied as to its tautness nodded to me.

"Thank you, Doctor, ever the obedient servant to your masters. Now, pick up the other coil please and pass to the inspector. Thank you. Now, please sit down in the chair opposite your dainty lady friend. I compliment you on your taste; she is a fine figure of a woman."

My blood boiled over and without pausing to consider my actions I rushed at Stapleton. He turned the pistol round in an instant and slammed the butt end into the side of my head. I was aware as I fell that Lestrade had made a threatening move towards Stapleton, but found the revolver turned on him.

74

"Now, gentlemen, no more heroics. Inspector, please bind the doctor in the manner you have seen."

"Sorry, Doctor," whispered the inspector as he bound me securely to the chair.

I looked up through bloodied eyes to see Beatrice silently weeping. I too mouthed the word 'sorry'.

Holmes, who until now had been strangely silent, spoke up, "Now the three of us are here at as your mercy, although I use the word advisedly, perhaps you would be good enough to release my brother and Mrs Heidler; they have done you no harm."

"Oh no, Mr Holmes I cannot do that, not yet. We have games to play, games that require partners. Oh yes, Inspector I know you have no one to play with, but I can rectify that."

"How do you mean, Stapleton?" asked Lestrade.

"My name is Baskerville, please address me as such. Remove your coat please. Thank you. Now your waistcoat. And finally, your cuffs."

"For what reason?"

"Just do it," he snarled. "Thank you."

While keeping the gun trained on us he picked up a glass container which had been sitting on the table.

"What do you think of my pet, gentlemen?" and passed the container in front of us. Sitting, almost hidden in one of the corners was a small spider with stripes on its body.

"You see how kind I am, Inspector. I have brought a playmate for you, except of course the playing may be somewhat short lived and indeed one-sided. Hold out your right arm please. Now, if you please inspector or would you perhaps prefer a bullet in your brain before the games commence?"

Lestrade held his arm out, terror etched upon his features, "You devil," he hissed.

"Quite so, Inspector, how correct you are. Let me tell you something about our little friend here. He loves to explore and he *will* explore you, rest assured of that; his legs will dance gaily across your skin until the urge to bite becomes too much for him to bear. You will be aware of a pin prick on your skin and then you will lose the power of your limbs. You will fall as a paralysis takes over your body and the pain spreads. Your limbs will no longer obey you, you voice will fly from your mouth. But your mind will remain sharp and you will know exactly what is happening to you and more importantly to me, who is doing it to you."

He held Lestrade's hand out and held his wrist firmly. He shook the spider out onto his wrist. We watched in horror as the spider scuttled under Lestrade's shirt cuff and disappeared from view. He stood there swaying a little, but unable to speak.

"Can you feel the delicate touches of its legs upon your skin? When they stop, well I have already explained to you what happens then. You may have five minutes left to you, maybe more; it all depends on your deadly playmate. So, gentlemen your good friend has his little friend to play with. Who wants to play next?"

"Stop this madness, Stapleton," cried Holmes, "if you wish revenge against us, then take it, but stop this torture."

"My revenge will come, Mr Holmes, but until then you really must allow me to indulge myself and do not call me Stapleton, have I not made myself clear on that point?"

"I will not besmirch a great family name, Stapleton," said Holmes defiantly, his eyes blazing.

Stapleton advanced on a restrained and helpless Holmes and drawing back his arm unleashed a punch of great ferocity, hitting Holmes squarely in the face. At once Holmes's nose erupted with a flow of blood.

"Now, Doctor Watson, I believe your beloved Beatrice wishes to play her part in today's sport. Let's see what we can find for her. Oh yes, I have the very thing." He picked up a narrow oblong box which had a number of holes bored into its lid.

"I can only afford you the briefest of glimpses, Doctor, but I am sure that will be all you require to recognise this old friend of yours."

He drew back the lid momentarily and allowed me to peep inside. I recoiled in horror at the deadly contents.

"Ah, I see recognition in your features. If you lived to write this up no doubt you would call it rather unimaginatively, 'The Return of the Swamp Adder'. Unfortunately, of course your writing career has come to an unexpected end and your readers will have to do without this particular tale although they will have the pleasure of reading your obituary. That, I feel will have to satisfy them."

Thrusting his hand inside the box he pulled out the snake by its rear extremity and in one movement threw it onto Beatrice's lap. She let forth an involuntary scream as the snake began to slither about her body. I struggled against my binds for all I was worth, cursing Stapleton all the while.

"Do not fret so, Doctor, the snake may not care to bite such dainty flesh. See, even now it heads for the floor and freedom. Of course, I do not wish to deprive it of the merits of so warm a body so perhaps I should impede its bolt for liberty and allow it once more to wander over Mrs Heidler as it pleases. There is an alternative, however. Would you care to know what it is?"

"Tell me," I cried, "damn you to hell, tell me."

"The fair Mrs Heidler can escape the fatal and extremely painful bite of this serpent if she agrees to suffer a far less painful death by my hands."

"If it saves John, I would agree to it. Take my life for his," she begged in an outpouring of such love as I had ever known.

"You are in no position to bargain, alas. However, I will spare *your* life if you act for me in one thing."

"What is that?" she asked this fiend.

"Oh, it's simplicity itself my dear, you shoot your beloved doctor yourself then you have my word that I will set you free."

"Never, never," she cried.

"Then you will both die. He picked up the snake and threw it onto Beatrice's shoulder, "there, so close to your pretty little neck."

A sudden movement to my left caught everyone's attention. Lestrade gave a little sigh and began swaying and then toppled to the floor. His limbs were undergoing convulsions and then he laid still, his breathing shallow, his eyes wide open and staring vacantly.

Stapleton walked over to where his prostrate form lay. "How does it feel to die, Inspector? Then Stapleton performed a pirouette and jumped in the air clapping his hands together triumphantly. "I never could have known just how sweet revenge could be, it is a positive boon to my soul." As he turned to walk away from Lestrade he aimed a kick into his ribs.

"You monster! Let the man die in peace now at least," I screamed at him.

Stapleton ignored me and watched the swamp adder's progress. It was still sitting on Beatrice's shoulder almost as if it was aware of the game's high stakes and was deliberating on its next move.

"While we wait for the snake to decide on Mrs Heidler's fate, let's involve Mycroft, I'm sure he is eager to join in."

"I am not a game player and if you wish to prolong the agony of all here then kindly do it without me. Shoot me like the coward you are. Or are you not man enough to do so?" said Mycroft.

"A Holmes with some fight in him unlike your young brother who sits there resigned to his fate. How exquisite."

"No more talk. Put a bullet in my brain and have done with it. Act like a man for once in your life."

"If you are so eager to meet your Maker then who am I to stand in your way? You are right, Mycroft Holmes. I am tired. The time for game playing is over."

He put his revolver against Mycroft's temple and as he did so, Mycroft nodded to his brother, not in a resigned way, but almost conspiratorially. I looked away, but there came no explosion, no loud report, just a series of barren clicks as Stapleton tried time and time again to discharge the gun.

"Your bullets may be found scattered along the lanes of Devonshire," said Mycroft quite coolly, "your telegram concerning my brother raised my suspicions immediately. There was something about it that did not ring true. These suspicions became much more definite when on our ride to this god-forsaken place I noticed the revolver in your overcoat pocket. I took the liberty of removing it and then making certain adjustments to its contents."

"Your joy will be short lived. How amusing it will be to kill you with the very revolver your brother brought here to use against me," he snarled.

Laughing maniacally, he strode across the room towards the hall. As he passed the still form of Lestrade, the inspector's arms shot out and his hands grabbed Stapleton's ankles and brought him down to the floor. Stapleton kicked out wildly and managed to free one leg, still Lestrade held on despite receiving a savage kick to his face. I was aware of Holmes struggling to free himself; I had tied my knots in such a way as to deceive Stapleton, but would enable the bonds to be broken with just a little effort. Stapleton aimed another kick at Lestrade and with an almighty effort got to his feet and ran into the hall. He returned with my service revolver and aimed it at Lestrade, determined to vent his fury on him. A shot rang out, but not from Stapleton. Holmes had loosened the binds on his wrists and in his hand was a derringer pistol. His shot had sent the revolver spinning from Stapleton's grasp. Now the hunter truly became the hunted. Stapleton took to his heels and we heard the sound of the front door being flung open.

Holmes snatched the snake away from Beatrice's shoulder and flung it into the fire. He undid the ropes which held me. "Come, Watson, we must end this fellow's villainy. I am sorry," he said to Beatrice and Mycroft, "we will loosen you shortly."

Holmes paused only to collect the revolver from the floor and we rushed out into the gloom of the afternoon followed by a battered and bloodied Lestrade. The distant figure of Stapleton could be seen heading towards the Grimpen mire, hoping to negotiate those pathways between the green-scummed pits and foul quagmires.

Holmes had undoubtedly gained on him a little; he was covering the ground far more quickly than we could ever hope to.

We heard a muffled shout somewhere ahead of us and as the mist cleared a little we could see Holmes sitting against the trunk of one of the stunted trees to be found on the moor.

"Are you all right, Holmes?" I shouted, "have you lost him?"

"No, he is here, Watson."

And then we saw. In a patch of the quivering mire was Stapleton. He was covered up to his thighs and although he knew better than to struggle it was clear he would sink inexorably into this bog-hole unless we could reach him. I looked at the tree for a branch long enough to reach the man, but Holmes touched my wrist as if to stay me.

"Help me, Mr Holmes, for pity's sake, help me," screamed Stapleton.

"We have to do something, Holmes. Regardless of what he has done he is a fellow human being."

"I will help you, Stapleton," called Holmes to the stricken man and calmly pointed the revolver at him and pulled the trigger. There was a momentary flicker of fear on Stapleton's face before the bullet tore into his skull.

"Holmes!" but I could say no more, not knowing how to bring forth my jumbled thoughts.

"*Exitus acta probat*," quoted Holmes. "Lestrade, I have shot a man in cold blood as you have just witnessed. I surrender myself to your custody."

"I missed the incident entirely, Mr Holmes. It appears at the crucial moment I was looking away. I believe Doctor Watson was also distracted."

"Thank you, Lestrade. You are the most loyal of men."

Holmes continued to sit there completely immobile as the minutes ticked by and the body of Stapleton continued its inexorable journey to the bottom of the mire. He only stirred finally when the body of that cruel and cold-hearted man was lost to view forever.

"Enough. It is over," he pronounced.

Chapter Eleven

We released Beatrice and Mycroft from their bonds and she fell into my arms, weeping.

"Oh John, thank God. I was convinced we would all die."

"So was I, to be truthful. I hoped that Holmes would be able to free himself, but even then I was not clear as to how we could stop the man."

"Were it not for the spider having taken an obvious dislike to Lestrade's skin then the outcome may well have been different." Holmes said.

"I could hardly believe it myself when the spider dropped out onto the floor; it was then I gave that small exclamation of surprise which fortunately Stapleton misread as something else. I endeavoured to sway directly over where the spider was motionless on the floor and my fall had the effect of crushing it. I knew that playing dead may well give me the chance to act and thanks to Mr Holmes's cunning and bravado so it proved."

"It was a dangerous game you played there, Mycroft."

"Undoubtedly, Sherlock, but I had the distinct impression you could use some assistance."

"A little maybe and Mrs Heidler," Holmes said, turning to Beatrice, "you are a brave lady and I would have expected nothing less from you. You and Watson are a formidable team and I am indeed fortunate to have you both as my very good friends. I think it's time that we returned to Lyme for a much needed rest."

The mystery of the missing Mr Glanvill and his family was solved by the simple expediency of asking at the post office. They had gone back home on receipt of a letter informing them of a severe illness to one of their parents; no doubt the work of Stapleton, but at least they were unharmed. It was early evening when we eventually arrived back at Exeter station ready for the connection to Axminster. Mycroft declared that he would be heading straight back to London to resume his orderly routine and in due course we said our goodbyes to that most remarkable man when we duly disembarked at Axminster.

"I wonder what drove Stapleton to these desperate crimes of vengeance," I asked Holmes later that evening.

"I don't think we can ever be certain of that. He no doubt always possessed a cruel streak and he acquired a taste for killing which had gone on unabated, probably for many years, possibly including the three boys who met their deaths at the school in Yorkshire where Stapleton was master. I am sure that if we had the inclination we could seek out information that would tell us where he had been these last nine years. I do not have that inclination however. Let him and his memory rot."

"Amen to that, Holmes."

At some point in the evening the enormity of the day and all the feelings and emotions it had brought to the surface caught up with us and sleep was the antidote for us all. My sleep was mercifully free of nightmares and was peaceful and as deep as I had hoped for.

In the morning there was a measured calm in the air. There were mundane tasks to be done such as letting Sergeant Street know the outcome to this grisly case. Lestrade and Holmes made arrangements to travel back to London together during the course of the evening. As our time and thoughts had been somewhat occupied since the inspector's arrival here, Holmes and I, together with Beatrice, elected to give Lestrade a hurried tour of Lyme Regis, taking in as much of the history and the charm of the place we could possibly manage in the time allotted to us.

It became apparent when we returned to Beatrice's that someone had been very busy in our absence. The aroma that greeted us was both divine and tempting beyond measure.

"Lydia has been a little angel and has prepared something especially for you, John," Beatrice said, smiling.

"I think you should sit down, old fellow before you fall down," said Holmes.

"I sat myself down at the table, with the keenest of anticipatory smiles spreading across my face.

Lydia walked into the room with a fork in one hand and a spoon in the other. These she placed in front of me reverently as though they were holy relics. She smiled sweetly and gave me the briefest of winks before departing for the kitchen. She returned moments later with a plate bearing a treasure which had a silver cover over it; this she removed to reveal the most exquisite plum pudding I think I had ever seen. I picked up the fork and spoon and shaking my head to myself wistfully, I walked over to the window, opened it, looked up and down the street and then closed it firmly. I walked into the hall, took a few steps to the door and locked and bolted it. I reclaimed my seat and picked up my fork and spoon anew. I brought the first spoonful to my mouth, savoured the moment and partook of a mouthful, not caring that all eyes were on me.

"Well," asked Lydia, "what do you think?"

"What do I think?"

"Yes," she repeated, "what do you think?"

I looked up into her brown eyes and gave her the broadest and the happiest of smiles.

"Life is good," I said.

Epilogue

Data Data Data!!! As Holmes would have put it. What evidence is there to suggest that this is a genuine adventure penned by Watson? Indeed, that any of these events actually happened as so described? I will expand on these points to the best of my ability:

What evidence is there?

As with the *'Lyme Regis Horror'* actual evidence and plain facts are thin on the ground. I could not trace any local newspaper records from 1898, however in a later edition of the *Lyme Regis News* dated July 16th 1906 there is a reference to a Scotland Yard inspector being sent to Lyme to assist in what is described as a 'domestic incident'. It reads in part:

'........readers may recall the last occasion when we played host to Scotland Yard when an Inspector Lestrade was present to look into the violent deaths of local businessmen, Robert Fane and Henry Madders. It is worth noting that even with the aid of the celebrated amateur detective, Mr Sherlock Holmes, a further atrocity could not be prevented. That is not to say that we do not welcome the arrival in this instance of a man from Scotland Yard.........'

We know for certain then that Holmes was in Lyme along with Lestrade looking into these two murders. I recently came into possession of a small collection of trade directories for Lyme Regis covering the period 1895-1905. Madders and Fane, Solicitors are listed until 1898, after that date their address is occupied by a Gents Outfitters. The same directories list a Mrs Heidler's Boarding House as being in Coombe Street from 1895-1901. This equates well with the entry that I found in the church register showing the marriage of Nathaniel Heidler to Elizabeth Hill in 1901. It is my belief that after Nathaniel married Elizabeth, his mother gave up the boarding house and joined Watson in London where they married and resided in Queen

Anne Street, although I feel quite strongly that together they would have retired to Dorset.

I had no luck with any evidence pertaining to James Broderick. I travelled to Sampford Courtenay in the hope of uncovering a trail which may lead me to him, but I was completely out of luck, although the pint of cider in The New Inn went some way to consoling me! Nor could I find any record of Mrs Austin or any reference to any published works of hers.

Dr James Spurr was indeed the chief medical officer for the town in 1898 and was noted as being instrumental in bringing the water supply in Lyme to an acceptable level of cleanliness and safety. Rendall's, Henley's and Beer and sons all occupied premises in Broad Street as described.

Can we be sure that Watson penned this tale?

The short answer is of course, no. We cannot be certain nor will we ever be. The handwriting is extremely similar to the known examples of the good doctor's and as far I can tell is identical to the original *'Lyme Regis Horror'* manuscript that is in my possession. The paper and ink certainly seem to be bona fide Victorian, but of course that proves nothing in itself.

If Watson didn't pen this, then who did? Nathaniel himself could be a candidate, after all the notes were in his possession. He had a close association with Watson and may have wanted to tell a tale by replicating as close as he could, Watson's own style. If that was the case, then we would have to consider Nathaniel as the possible author of the *'Lyme Regis Horror'*. But then we come to the diary............

Where did the diary come from?

The diary is an untidy looking thing, pages torn out, false starts and lots of corrections. At times the nib has been pressed to paper so hard that the paper has ripped in several places. The handwriting is wayward and slants this way and that. I am fortunate to know a graphology expert, one of the best in his field, a Dr Michael Stammers, who was kind enough to examine the diary for me. It was to be fair, a very brief inspection, but from this he was able to tell me that he thought the writer was a middle aged man, right handed who was in a highly charged state when he put down these words. In Dr Stammers's opinion the man who wrote this diary had committed the acts he described or at the very least believed he had committed them. And was in the grip of a deep rooted mania.

It is odd admittedly that Watson does not mention this journal for if it is genuinely Stapleton's then it must have been found at Baskerville Hall and it must have one time been in Watson's possession for it then to pass to Nathaniel. My belief is that it is indeed Stapleton's diary and it is for that reason I used selective extracts from it at the end of each chapter.

The verdict?

Notwithstanding the difficulties, I believe the 'Lyme Regis Legacy' to be the work of Watson. I don't think he ever seriously considered publishing it; Holmes's act in despatching Stapleton would have precluded any such publication (although it could be construed a mercy killing). That episode could have been excised leaving readers with the death of Stapleton in the mire of course, but there are other reasons telling against its publication. Holmes would not have seen this as any kind of success owing to the deaths of Nanther and Broderick and there is not much work for Holmes to do by way of deductive processes as it's more or less a chase, 'the hunter and the hunted' as he puts it. 'The Hound of the Baskervilles' was not published until August 1901 and it's possible that Watson thought it better not to return the readers to Baskerville Hall.

Empty speculation? Absolutely! As in all these previously unrecorded cases of Watson's, let the reader decide.

I cannot tell precisely how many more times I will pick up my pen to write of my friend Mr Sherlock Holmes, although I feel in my bones that this will indeed be the final occasion that I will record an account of the most remarkable man I have ever known. With Holmes's permission I had recently published some further exploits of his; fully intending that these will form the final collection of tales I will set before the public of the world's original and foremost private consulting detective.

Holmes still lived in quiet retirement on the Sussex downs far from the madding crowd, an ever quieter retirement than he even he may have anticipated due to events of five years ago. I remember well the terse telegram I had received from Martha, his housekeeper, informing me of a stroke that Holmes had suffered. I motored down to Fulworth in extreme anguish, fearful of what state I would find my closest friend in. His own physician was in attendance and informed me that although the stroke Holmes had been struck down with was severe, he was hopeful of at least a partial recovery, owing in part no doubt to Holmes's own indomitable spirit refusing to be vanquished.

Holmes's appearance brought a lump to my throat and a tear to my eyes. He endeavoured to stand to greet me, but his body refused to obey him, his left arm hung uselessly at his side. His attempts at speech were slurred and indistinct. My only thought was that this must be akin to a living death for Holmes to be so afflicted. He looked at me and then cast a mournful glance at his prized Stradivarius, acknowledging with his eyes that this and other parts of his life were now over.

I left Holmes later that day with a heavy heart fearful for my friend's very existence. I made promises to come and visit as often as I could, my own health permitting.

Fate intervened however and I was struck down with a heart attack not long after my return home; a warning too, that my time was also running out. My life was despaired of for several weeks and ruefully I considered that my life, like Holmes's own could now never be the same.

We exchanged many letters over the ensuing five years. Holmes had hung on all this time with the tenacity he had displayed throughout his time in practice, exercising his iron will in what would surely be his last battle. I was overjoyed to learn that there had indeed been a partial recovery in both senses and movement. My only regret was that I was unable to see this for myself, my own health being far too perilous to undertake such a journey.

Yesterday evening was spent in going through notes of old cases and putting them in some semblance of order. Although, as I have stated, I have no inclination of publishing any more of these accounts, I still felt driven to bury myself once more in the past, perhaps for no other reason than it gave me the greatest of pleasure to do so. I was on the point of giving up my labours for the night and retiring when I was disturbed by a loud knock at the door. I glanced at the clock on the mantel which told me it was well past 11pm, grumbling to myself I nevertheless headed down the hallway to receive my night-time visitor with certainly no inkling of who it could be. Imagine my utter surprise and joy to find Holmes on the doorstep, his grey eyes shining in the gloom like the sleuth-hound of old.

"How are you?" he said cordially, gripping my hand with a strength for which I should hardly have given him credit for, knowing how ill he had been.

"My dear fellow; how wonderful to see you? I can't believe it. This is beyond anything I could have expected. But are you sure you are well enough to have come all this way to see me?"

"Time is short, Watson. The game is afoot once more. Can you make yourself ready to accompany me, I have a cab waiting."

I dressed hurriedly, or as hurriedly as a man of seventy eight can and re-joined Holmes. We stepped out into a foggy and strangely silent street and into the cab.

"Where are we going, Holmes?"

"To a place you will know when you see it."

He said no more and we rushed on through deserted streets, the impenetrable fog made it well nigh impossible to recognise any familiar landmarks although I was aware we were travelling eastwards. Holmes stayed silent and did not elaborate on our destination or indeed what our reason for going there may be. The cab pulled up and asking the driver to wait for us Holmes led me into the darkness. We turned down a narrow lane and passed through a small side-door; which with a thrill I recognised as one that would lead us into a wing of Bart's, that revered, ancient hospital and national institution. I needed no guiding as we ascended the bleak stone staircase and made our way to the chemical laboratory where forty nine years before I had first encountered Mr Sherlock Holmes.

"Do you remember the scene, Watson?"

"As if it was only yesterday."

"And if you could by chance have your time over again, would you alter the decision you made that day to throw in your lot with me?"

"No, my decision would be the very same. But what on earth are we doing back here? Has a crime been committed?"

"No crime my friend, but a mystery, a mystery I have always striven to have the answer to and I feel now that I stand on the brink of solving it."

"What mystery, Holmes?"

He brushed my question aside and retraced his steps to the waiting cab as I followed in his wake, puzzling over Holmes's purpose in bringing me here. I puzzled too over the disquieting feeling that not only was he acting like the Holmes of old in spite of his ill-health, but the also the fact that he somehow looked younger. In fact I would have been ready to swear that he looked the same as he did all those years ago when he greeted me with the words "You have been in Afghanistan I perceive." I shook my head and muttered 'ineffable twaddle' under my breath.

"Drive on," Holmes commanded the driver, but gave him no directions to follow. A while later we pulled up outside a row of four houses set back from the street. One of these had an ill-omened and minatory look.

"It's Lauriston Gardens," I exclaimed.

"Yes, the scene of our first investigation together."

"I was more in the role of observer, Holmes."

"I concede that point to you. Nevertheless it marked the start of our partnership in earnest."

"Not exactly a partnership."

"Oh yes; a partnership, Watson. Have no doubts on that score."

"Why are we here, Holmes?"

"Because I wish it, Watson, because I wish it."

Holmes turned on his heels and returned to the cab, issued another barked, "Drive on." and settled back in the seat.

I sat beside him growing evermore perplexed by the night's events. I had never marked Holmes down as being overly nostalgic so there must be some purpose to what was occurring, but what? Holmes looked straight ahead as the cab traversed roads and streets, the driver seemingly oblivious to the dense fog which wrapped itself around us and drove as though it was the clearest of days. The silence in the cab was almost as marked as the silence outside. Though the fog was as thick as I had ever seen it, I managed to see the occasional glimpses of landmarks familiar to me; dear old Baker Street, Scotland Yard, Upper Swandam Lane, and the Northumberland Hotel. I gasped involuntarily as I caught sight of the Lyceum Theatre where the adventure of 'The Sign of Four' began in earnest which resulted in the bliss of matrimony for me. At this juncture Holmes planted his long, bony hand on my shoulder, an action which spoke volumes for his rarely seen humanity. After travelling for an hour or so in this manner during which many other familiar images revealed themselves to my sight and mind, the cab came to a halt once more. I peered through the gloom at an old fashioned Early Georgian edifice. I could make out two deep bay windows on the ground floor. Holmes lit a match and the light illuminated a small brass plate which bore the name, 'Garrideb'.

"Garrideb lives here still? Surely not."

"No," said Holmes gently.

I looked at the plate again. My mind must have been playing tricks on me for the name it bore was one of 'Stammers'. How I remembered that day long ago in 136 Little Ryder Street where I caught a glimpse of a great heart as well of that of a great brain. Holmes's clear, hard eyes were dimmed and his firm lips were shaking. As I glanced at Holmes now I saw that self-same look on his face.

"I put you in danger many times my friend and the pain I felt that day has never left me. I hope you can find it in your heart to forgive an old friend for his many thoughtless actions."

"There is nothing to forgive, Holmes. Absolutely nothing."

"Thank you my friend. It is time to go, I cannot tarry any longer. The driver will, I am sure, take you back to your house and your welcome bed whilst I make my way to the station."

"Why not stay with me, Holmes? I am sure you are as weary as I am."

"Yes, Watson, I am weary and it is for that very reason I must go."

"Then I will accompany you to the station and do not attempt to argue."

The station, when we reached it was bursting into life, porters hurrying and scurrying and early morning travellers beginning to fill the concourse. Holmes smiled at me and shook my hand firmly, but remained silent. I hardly knew what to say, the night having drained me completely so I remained silent too. I watched the tall, gaunt figure of my friend stride towards the train. Then he was gone, swallowed up completely by his fellow travellers and I saw him no more.

I made my way home in a melancholy frame of mind, but curiously uplifted too. I barely registered the fact that in spite of being out for several hours in an unusually thick fog, my clothes were bone dry. I slept fitfully with vivid dreams of a past I would never forget in association with a man I would never forget.

This morning, a telegram arrived.

He awoke with a jolt. Napping he had always thought of as Watson's province, but more and more it was becoming his own. His notes were spread all over the dining table, just another thing for Martha to complain about. His magnum opus was coming along slowly, but assuredly not surely. Truth be told the textbook he had promised to write for himself, but for the benefit of others, 'The Art of Detection' was fast becoming a millstone around his neck. He constantly questioned the necessity of such a book in this modern age, yet how else to fill his time? The hives had long since been sold off along with their contents. In the early years of his retirement he was still consulted by Scotland Yard detectives when they had been faced with particularly thorny and knotty problems. That was all a long, long time ago and now he was ignored and forgotten by the outside world. So here he was working uselessly at his book each and every day. Oh well so be it.

Even the good Watson had passed beyond his ken apart from very occasional visits. He could picture him now, living happily in retirement in Dorset. Watson had of course always been a more sociable creature than him and no doubt his life now consisted of golfing, dances, balls and all the social niceties of life. A twinge of rheumatism assailed him as it did more and more these days and he picked up his favourite pipe, threw a blanket over his shoulders and did as his doctor ordered, 'Fresh air, sea air, Mr Holmes' was that worthy fellow's mantra. Well there was an abundance of that just a few steps from his cottage......

****

He had been dreaming he was sure of it, but the dream receded back into his unconscious from whence it had come. Sleep which seemed so difficult by night had virtually imprisoned him by day. And just what did his days consist of? Going back over case notes of his time with Holmes. Reminiscing, re-visiting and writing them up as before. But now he questioned whether anybody would want to read them in this day and age, the world had moved on. He had not. He was reliving the past more and more, his copious notes were an ever present in his study. Every surface was covered with them, overflowing onto the floor; he had become more like Holmes than Holmes in that respect. How Holmes must be enjoying his retirement. No doubt there were still the constant calls from Scotland Yard appealing for his help; streams of detectives making their way to his door. A sudden pain shot through his side, his old wound and its attendant pain was an ever present these days. A spot of fresh air was called for, gathering up his coat, cap and pipe he headed for the door.

****

The view over the downs and out to sea was undoubtedly revitalising, but it had the effect of demoralising him also. The beauty and vitality of the scene before him contrasted sharply with the lonely life he led, the unremitting futility of his once cherished aim to produce the definitive textbook on crime detection. Breathing in the sea air, he sighed deeply. What was the point of feeling sorry for himself? He had lived his life in the manner he wanted, he had no regrets. He just felt there was something missing. Idly he wondered what Watson was doing now, not feeling sorry for himself certainly and Watson would no doubt be horrified to see his old friend like this.

****

The view before him was as lovely as ever. Whatever the weather or conditions he never failed to be inspired by the Dorset coast. He had this vista; he had his work such as it was. He should be happy. Was he? His life seemed to consist of memories only, faded yet brought to life by his notes. He had no real reason to feel sorry for himself; it did no good to think that way. Life had been good to him mostly, yet now he keenly felt there was something missing from it somehow. Holmes came into his thoughts unbidden; he very much doubted Holmes was feeling this way and he thought that in a strange way he was letting his old friend down.

****

He thrust his pipe into his pocket and walked the few steps to the door of his cottage. Pausing, he said out loud, '*Watson*', smiled and let himself in.

****

Shaking his head, he retraced his steps to his humble abode. Out of nowhere, rising up from within him, came the single word, '*Holmes*'. Smiling, he let himself in.

From the Journals of Doctor John H Watson

December 26th 1932

An anachronism, that's how I thought of myself yesterday whilst driving down to pay my annual visit to my old friend, Mr. Sherlock Holmes. An anachronism in a modern world, hardly flattering I know, but something I always feel quite keenly when visiting Holmes. We both belonged to another age, an age of gaslights, impenetrable London fogs and Hansom cabs rattling through London streets. The light had gone from my life when Holmes decided to retire permanently to Sussex and I was more aware than ever that at eighty years of age, I was marking time. Marking time down to the inevitable, the one mystery that even Holmes declared he could not solve. Christmas had a special significance for me in relation to Holmes and with no other distractions to hold me; I made my annual pilgrimage to see Holmes on Christmas Day itself. It may be that pilgrimage is the wrong word, but, no, it seems just right to me on reflection. My respect and brotherly love for Holmes did indeed border on veneration.

Driving for me these days is a somewhat onerous task. The pace of modern life on our roads leaves me both breathless and confused and I resolved to make yesterday's visit the last one, the final one to my old friend. As always on these occasions, I thought back to the adventures Holmes and I had shared and for the whole of the journey from my own house to Holmes's, I was young again, revitalised with the years falling away from me.

The snow was beginning to fall as I arrived on that familiar scene. I opened up the weather-beaten old gate and walked over to my friend. I had brought a small Christmas offering of seasonal flowers and these I placed beneath the headstone. I looked down with pride as I read the words.....

S.Holmes

Born January 6th 1854

Died December 25th 1927

'Fearless'

'A loyal and good friend'

I tried to put into words that I could visit no more, but speech would not come. Yet, I had made certain arrangements to ensure that my resting place would be my friend's side as it always was. Together for all eternity.

As I turned to go, my voice came back to me, "Soon, my friend, soon."

Editor's note:

This was the last entry in Dr. Watson's Journal. His housekeeper found his lifeless body the following morning. It was reported that he was lying peacefully on his side, a smile on his face and an arm outstretched as though in the act of greeting or being greeted.

The Locked Room Mystery

The last few months of 1896 following our return from Dorset had been an extremely busy and fruitful time for my friend Mr Sherlock Holmes. Cases came and went with bewildering speed; some were worked on concurrently with Holmes's customary brilliance. I particularly recall the adventure of The Man with Three Feet and the havoc he wrought in Kentish Town, whilst the same area brought us into contact with the machinations of the alliteratively named Colonel Charles Chamberlain who so nearly brought the government to its knees. 'A worthy successor to Moriarty' was how Holmes described him which gives some measure of the man and his evil.

During this time I was acutely worried about Holmes's health. As he threw himself into these cases he resumed his usual pattern of frenetic activity, little sleep and lack of food. As Holmes saw it as his right that I should be by his side (which I was, as always) I too suffered sleepless nights and interruptions to my daily routine. My own constitution was nowhere near as strong as my friend's and indeed both it and I were close to breaking point, a fact that seemed not to be recognised by Holmes as his singular commitment and devotion to the tasks at hand occupied him fully.

All these recent cases had been initially introduced to us by Inspector Lestrade and he too had been expected to join Holmes and me at all hours of the day and night in pursuance of these singular crimes. Lestrade could hardly complain at this as he had his professional standing to protect, hence his appealing to Holmes in the first instance.

Nevertheless he confided in me just a few days ago that, 'he was thoroughly and completely exhausted'.

On this particular November morning we had breakfasted in silence save for the normal everyday pleasantries that two old friends may be expected to share. I was fervently hoping that now Holmes's caseload had begun to lessen I may have time to myself once more. I was acutely aware how much I needed it. The silence was broken by the ringing of the door bell.

"A confident and insistent ring," said Holmes, "at this hour it can only be the telegram boy from Wigmore Street office."

"It could be a client, Holmes. It is not unknown for us to receive visitors at this hour."

"True, my friend, but if that were the case we may expect the pushing of the door bell to be somewhat more hesitant. No, a telegram it is."

Mrs Hudson duly delivered a telegram a few moments later.

"Ah", exclaimed Holmes as he tore it open and perused its contents, "it is from Lestrade. 'A VERY SINGULAR MURDER.STOP.NORTHUMBERLAND HOTEL.STOP.IN URGENT NEED OF YOUR HELP.STOP'.

"Well it would seem Lestrade is out of his depth once more. Gulp down your coffee Watson and let us go and give our friend the inspector a helping hand."

I surveyed the portions of breakfast that remained untouched, but a look from Holmes told me that any protest would be futile so once more I put my weary limbs into action and with an air of resignation fetched my hat and coat.

A short while later we encountered Lestrade in the plush foyer of the Northumberland Hotel, looking not only puzzled, but dejected too, "Good morning Mr Holmes, Doctor. Well here we are again gentleman, another puzzle and a right pretty one it is too. We need to go up to the fifth floor so I will apprise you both while we ascend."

"Excellent, Lestrade. Be thorough and omit nothing however inconsequential it may seem."

"Don't you think I know that by now, Mr Holmes? Well, it seems a gentleman going by the name of Thaddeus Grimshaw booked into the hotel yesterday evening. He announced that he would be staying for two days. Rather oddly he had no luggage with him of any description."

"Perhaps it was going to be forwarded later from another hotel," Holmes opined.

"Be that as it may Mr Holmes, he will certainly have no need of it now."

"Tch tch, Lestrade. You are just like Watson who has a fondness for telling his stories hindmost first. Proceed logically please."

Lestrade drew himself up to his not overly impressive height and continued.

"Mr Grimshaw ordered enough food and drinks to sustain him for his proposed two day residence and expressly asked not to be disturbed. To that end he placed one of the hotel's 'Do Not Disturb' signs on his door knob and no more was heard from him.

Around seven o'clock this morning what seemed to be like a pistol shot was heard by other guests on the fifth floor. The duty manager duly responded, one Mr Alfred Wilson. He gained entrance to room 519 by means of a spare key which is kept in the reception of the hotel."

"I take it although the room was locked that the key that Mr Grimshaw used was no longer in the lock?" asked Holmes.

"Correct, in fact that key was nowhere to be found, but I will come to that point soon gentlemen. On entering the room Mr Wilson was met with the hideous sight of Mr Grimshaw face down on the carpet with a bullet hole in his back and quite obviously dead."

"Did he have the presence of mind to search the suite?" Holmes asked.

"No, but he did have the presence of mind to beat a hasty retreat making sure to lock the door on his exit. As chance would have it there was a constable engaged on his beat who was passing by the hotel at that time. He accompanied the duty manager up to the room and with Mr Wilson guarding the door he searched the entire suite. There was no one else there nor indeed any place that anyone could conceal themselves."

"Is there a fire escape?"

"No, Mr Holmes, just a sheer drop to the pavement from each window."

"A bullet in the back would tend to exclude any notion of suicide. A pretty puzzle indeed as you said, Lestrade."

"Ah, but Mr Holmes there are more oddities to come. As I mentioned, the key to the room was missing. There was no weapon and by the side of the body lying next to the dead man's right hand was a note. It had just two words on it; it read, 'TWO DAYS'."

"Have you ascertained how many keys there are for this room?"

"Just the two; the one that Mr Grimshaw took with him into the room and the one that Mr Wilson collected from reception."

"Tell me Lestrade, were there any signs that there had been a visitor to the room other than Mr Wilson, the police constable, you, the departed guest and anyone else you may have invited in?"

"None that I could see."

"Which means next to nothing of course," Holmes rejoined.

Lestrade ignored this unnecessary slight on Holmes's part and motioned us to step out of the lift as we had now reached the fifth floor. The corridor was dimly lit, but our destination was made clear to us by a burly police constable standing to attention outside room 519. Holmes looked at him closely as if he knew him, perhaps having met him during another case I thought.

"Excuse me," said Holmes, "but did you not used to be in the detective branch? Sergeant Clark isn't it?"

"Bless me sir, no. My name is Smithers and I fear promotion to sergeant is something I will never see."

"My mistake then," said Holmes, "but I could have sworn...." Turning to Lestrade he asked, "Do you not see the resemblance to Clark, who was with you on the Wapping case in 1890?"

"Maybe a little, Mr Holmes, but as it has nothing to do with our present mystery I fail to see why you attach any import to it."

"No importance, Lestrade. Just one of those coincidences which seem to litter our lives. A mere whimsy of mine. Now then, has everything been left as it was found? I take it the body itself has not been moved or otherwise disturbed?"

"Sad to say....it has."

"What!!!???" cried Holmes, "You of all people should realise the importance of not tampering with the integrity of a crime scene. Good God man, how could you allow this to happen?"

"Please hear me out Mr Holmes. Now, Smithers has been on duty outside since his inspection of the room. The one key we have is in his possession. Now, Smithers please confirm to these gentlemen that you have not left your post for an instant nor has anyone gained admittance."

"That's correct, sir. I sent Mr Wilson to call the Yard while I remained here."

"And once again, Smithers; you have remained here on duty throughout that time and no one has been admitted to the room nor has anyone left the room?"

"Bless me sir, there wouldn't be anyone to leave the room would there?" he answered chuckling away.

"Smithers!" warned Lestrade, "please answer my questions without all this tomfoolery."

"Sorry sir. No, as I said before, I have not left my post and no one has been admitted to the room."

"Excellent, Lestrade. We have established that PC Smithers is a most dedicated officer which is entirely admirable I am sure, but pray tell me how does that advance us?"

"Only this, Mr Holmes, there is no longer a body in this room!" Lestrade announced as he flung open the door.

"Great God in heaven," I cried, "that's impossible!"

105

"Nevertheless, Doctor, there it is. Or in this case perhaps I should say there it isn't." Lestrade said, unexpectedly breaking into laughter at his own joke.

Holmes had flung himself onto the floor in the region of the very clear bloodstain, every fibre of his being suddenly alert. While Holmes was examining the room and its contents in the minutest of detail, Mr Wilson had entered and was engaging in a most earnest conversation with Lestrade.

"Unless the management of this establishment are playing a monstrous trick upon us for reasons of their own then this is a mystery truly worthy of your talents, Holmes," I said.

He paid no heed to this comment of mine, but focused his attentions on the note with its cryptic message, *TWO DAYS* after a few moments spent thus he threw away the note with an exclamation of, "Nothing, nothing!"

"I am momentarily at a loss, gentlemen. Why did Mr Grimshaw have such need of privacy? His ordering of the ample food and drink tells us that he fully intended not to leave the room for two days. But what does this note mean? Did he write it? Did another? Was there an assignation planned? Was he fearful for his life? It seems most probable given the events that followed. Is there a connection between Wilson and Grimshaw? Or anyone else in the hotel?"

"I can answer at least one of your questions Mr Holmes. There may well be a connection between Wilson and Mr Grimshaw, but not a connection that could have been acted upon for Wilson was at his post all night, other members of the staff have confirmed this to me."

"And the other question of course is where the body is now? How came it to leave the room?"

"Yes indeed, Watson."

"Holmes, would you like some time to yourself to ponder these questions? It seems to me to be somewhat more than a three pipe problem."

"A course of action I was about to suggest. Thank you, Watson."

"Very well, we will leave you to your pondering. Perhaps it would be as well if I locked the door Holmes to try and replicate the conditions of the crime as closely as possible."

"An excellent suggestion," he said as he removed a pipe and a quantity of shag from an inner pocket.

Lestrade and I left the room together. Smithers was no longer outside the door having gone to resume his other duties. I placed the 'Do Not Disturb' sign on the door knob.

"Well, Doctor. Where now?"

"I was thinking that lunch at Goldinis would not be out of place and this afternoon I rather fancy going to the 'Egyptian Hall' in Bond Street. David Devant has created a new illusion which is the talk of the town and old Mr Maskelyne himself is performing on the bill, I believe."

"An afternoon of magic, mystery and illusion sounds just the thing for two jaded souls. And tomorrow?"

"My dear Lestrade; tomorrow will be your choice entirely."

"Best foot forward then, Doctor."

"One moment, there is something I have forgotten." I retraced my steps to the door of room 519 and taking a pencil from my pocket I scribbled beneath 'Do Not Disturb' the extra words,..........'for two days'.

An Ode to Sherlock Holmes (written in the style of William McGonagall)

Hail! Sherlock Holmes in praise of you I will write if I may

For you smite the criminal classes without the least fear or delay

Hail! Sherlock Holmes for like you there is no other

Excepting maybe Mycroft your older brother

I can picture you both on the knee of your beloved mother.

Hail! Sherlock Holmes of thee I now commence my lay

And I do this most gladly without fear or dismay

You share your life with Doctor Watson a man most humble and fair

With whom you made your home in Baker Street, a most pleasant thoroughfare

Where the citizens of London stroll daily without a care.

Hail! Sherlock Holmes I thrilled to your story A Study in Scarlet

It gladdened my heart for in this tale there was no harlot.

Because it has to be said from all such vices you abstain

Excepting your deplorable occasional use of cocaine

But rejoice! You have seen the light and will use it never again.

Hail! Sherlock Holmes in praise of you I write this humble ode

Because it is simpler to read than the Dancing Men code.

For I have to say your triumphs are known far and wide

For on the side of righteousness you do side

And for this reason many a criminal from you would hide.

Hail! Sherlock Holmes the good and mighty detective

For in my view you are not at all defective.

You dealt most ably with that dreadful hound

When all around danger was to be found

And your reasoning in this case was most sound.

Hail! Sherlock Holmes how sad I was with your death at Reichenbach Falls

Which caused my heart to be as heavy as any stone built walls.

Then to see you come to life again was most grand

Once more on the side of right to stand

And your name rang once more throughout the land.

Hail! Sherlock Holmes I declare your wits are so keen

The finest detective I venture to say the world has ever seen.

To jail many worthless felons you sent

Which no doubt caused them a little discontent

But I live in hope the sinners will repent.

Hail! Sherlock Holmes the master of all things logical

In the opinion of your humble poet the great McGonagall.

Over the criminal classes you hold sway

By proving their guilt without delay

And it has to be said without fear or dismay.

Hail! Sherlock Holmes of thee my pen cannot refuse to write

For you have put many an evil man to flight

And in conclusion let me venture to say

That crime will happen by night and by day

But hail! Sherlock Holmes for you are the best detective in the world at the present day.

William Topaz McGonagall *(March 1825 – 29 September 1902) was a Scottish weaver, poet and actor. He won notoriety as an extremely bad poet who exhibited no recognition of or concern for his peers' opinions of his work. He wrote some 200 poems, including the infamous "Tay Bridge Disaster", which are widely regarded as some of the worst in British history. Groups throughout Scotland engaged him to make recitations from his works; contemporary descriptions of these performances indicate that many of these listeners were appreciating McGonagall's skill as a comic music hall character, and as such his readings may be considered a form of performance art. Collections of his verse continue in popularity, with several volumes available today.*

McGonagall has been acclaimed as the worst poet in British history. The chief criticisms of his poetry are that he is deaf to poetic metaphor and unable to scan correctly. In the hands of lesser artists, this might generate merely dull, uninspiring verse. McGonagall's fame stems from the humorous effects these shortcomings generate. The inappropriate rhythms, weak vocabulary, and ill-advised imagery combine to make his work amongst the most spontaneously amusing comic poetry in the English language. His is a long tradition of verses written and published about great events and tragedies, and widely circulated among the local population as handbills. In an age before radio and television, their voice was one way of communicating important news to an avid public.

"She will not return, Watson. Forgive my bluntness."

I had been pacing the room for some time now and Holmes could hardly have failed to notice my agitation. It had been a few short months since my dear wife had departed this life and with it being the evening of October 31st when boundaries between the spirit world and the living become somewhat blurred, I was hopeful of a sign of any kind that Mary was at peace. Was I expecting a visitation? I cannot in all conscience say yes, but how sweet it would be to gaze on her likeness once more.

"Your analytical reasoning may lead you to such a conclusion Holmes, but I am a creature of emotion and passion."

"And if you were to see a phantom of your late wife, how could you be sure it was not a phantasm of the brain projected onto your surroundings by your grief and your need?"

"Perhaps I would not be sure. Either way, Holmes I would be comforted beyond measure and my grief assuaged."

"To be blunt with you Watson, the dead do not walk the earth. Their shades do not return either to comfort or assuage."

"I need to believe and your coldness at a time like this does you no credit at all if I may speak bluntly too."

"Oh, Watson. My abject apologies if you perceive me as cold. I care about you, my dear fellow and what this folly may do to you. Halloween and its origins are now so shrouded in mystery that we cannot be sure that it had anything to do with spirits and the like. And besides if ghosts truly existed why would they need to wait until an arbitrarily appointed day on the calendar to appear?"

"There is an element of truth in what you say, Holmes, but spirits and revenants have appeared in their multitudes over the years. Can all the eye-witnesses to these supernatural sights and sounds have been mistaken? I believe firmly that we have a soul and this soul survives in some fashion and can reveal itself to us, perhaps only in time of great need."

"The soul returns then in the guise of its former body then is the gist of what you say, Watson?"

"Yes."

"Do clothes have souls then? Why do not these spirits return to us naked?"

"It may be a question of propriety, Holmes."

"Oh, Watson it will not do, it really won't."

"Then how do you account for the tales of ghosts spanning thousands of years be it Halloween or any other time?"

"I have to admit that I have not given it a great deal of thought over the years and I have no data to enable me to come to conclusions in individual cases, but I do have a theory of my own, Watson. Namely, that ghosts are not, as I have expressed, the dead coming back to walk among us, but rather they are living, breathing human beings."

"Preposterous, Holmes. How could that be?"

"Bear with me. If we look at time as a continuous loop then we can surely perceive of times when that loop can become misshapen through some universal mischance and folds in on itself. I believe the result of this is a time anomaly whereby a window of sorts opens up and enables some people to see what is happening in a bygone time for a short while."

"It seems to me to be outlandish in the extreme, but we will have to agree to differ on this occasion Holmes. For me ghosts are indeed the spirits of the dead and this is something I will always believe."

"My final words on the subject, painful as they might be to you on this All Hallows Eve are that there are no such things as ghosts. I would stake the whole of any reputation I may have garnered over the years on that statement."

We resumed our sitting in silence. My heart was still full of longing and I knew rest would not come easily to me. The silence seemed to grow even more marked and I was dimly aware that my name was being called, faintly as though whispered in the wind. The gas lights dimmed and flickered creating dancing shadows on the walls for an instant. Then I was aware of another shadow which appeared to me to step out of the very fabric of the wall itself. This shadow grew more substantial by the second, changing rapidly until my own sweet Mary stood before me. Radiant and beautiful just as in life.

113

"I have little time, John. I wish you peace and please take very good care of yourself. I love you now as I did then."

I have no clear recollection of my response to these words. I told her I loved her and always would, I know that much. Within a few seconds she had faded once more into the shadows and melted into the wall from whence she had come. I was overcome for more than a few minutes and had given little thought to Holmes while this extraordinary event was unfolding. However, as I glanced at him now; I saw a man in shock, his mouth open, his eyes staring at that point on the wall where the image of my Mary had appeared. I poured my friend a large brandy and brought it to his lips. I brought my mouth to his ear.

"Norbury," I whispered.

Easter in Lyme (suggested by Watson's 'Lyme Regis Legacy' manuscript)

The spring of 1899 brought me back down to Lyme Regis once again. It was by then three years since I had made my first visit there in the company of my friend, Mr. Sherlock Holmes. We had been invited to spend some time with my old friend and colleague Dr. Godfrey Jacobs, but instead of the pleasant holiday we had been expecting, or at least I had been expecting, we came up against a quite unimaginable horror, a tale so shocking it will never see the light of day. (Editor's *note: In fact a record of this adventure has recently come to light in Lyme Regis itself and is has been published as 'The Lyme Regis Horror').*

That visit also introduced me to the beautiful Mrs Beatrice Heidler and we had formed a wonderful and close association which we fully expected to result in marriage when the time was right. Mrs Heidler ran a guest house in Coombe Street in Lyme and for the sake of propriety I no longer stayed at her establishment when I made the journey down, but instead sought out other quarters. Latterly I had stayed with Dr Jacobs and his charming family, but as this family had grown by one since the occasion of my last visit, this was no longer possible. Instead, I had taken up an invitation from the Coade family to stay at their delightful residence Belmont House which commanded great views of the Cobb and the sea from its lofty position. The invitation I had so kindly received was extended to Sherlock Holmes and I was greatly surprised when he announced his intention to take up said invitation. He was due to arrive in two days time when Easter would be upon us. In the meantime, inspired by the all encompassing beauty of this place I elected to try my hand at extending my writing beyond that of cataloguing my friend's cases.

I had stumbled across an oft told story of an event which had taken place here. A local woman had fallen for a French naval officer who had then deserted her. The tale related how she would stand desolate and forlorn at the end of the Cobb, awaiting in vain his return. I compiled copious notes on the subject and came up with a title for the tale, 'The Strange Affair of The Woman and The French Officer ', but quickly realised it would take a better writer than me to do full justice to the story. (Editor's *note: The author John Fowles became a later resident of Belmont House, would it be too fanciful to suggest that he may have come across Watson's notes from nearly 70 years before?*)

I spent the rest of my time before Holmes's arrival both with Beatrice and her son Nathaniel and in solitude, marvelling as I always did in the splendours of this pearl of the South coast. Nothing ever seemed to change in Lyme; the beauties I had first encountered here were the beauties I encountered now. As Easter began I met Holmes at Axminster station with a dog cart for the six mile trip back into Lyme.

"My word, Watson," he enthused," it's quite remarkable what a change comes over you when you visit this place, you are looking most radiant."

"Thank you, Holmes and I trust your stay here will have the same result for you," I replied.

"We will see, we will see."

We rode down to Lyme in companionable silence, for my part in complete contentment. Holmes seemed preoccupied and I had no doubts he was reflecting on his previous visit here. I was gratified to find my deductions were correct.

"Tell me Watson, has anything been heard further of a certain *friend* of ours?" he asked warily.

"No, Holmes, nothing"

The reader will forgive me this only allusion to what we encountered nigh on three years ago, but neither Holmes nor I could ever expect to throw off the shackles of that evil time. After we settled in at Belmont House, we strolled down Sherborne Lane and from there to Monmouth House the home of Dr. Jacobs, his wife Sarah and their three children; Arthur, Cecil and Violet.

"Mr. Holmes, so good to see you again" said Jacobs, "and if you have no objections, the children have a mystery they wish you to solve."

Holmes laughed in that peculiar silent fashion of his, "No objections at all, my dear fellow."

Holmes and Jacobs then spent a short time in a most earnest discussion, following which the children came in. Violet was taken away by Sarah for an afternoon nap and Arthur and Cecil outlined their problem to Holmes.

Arthur spoke first, "Mr. Holmes, Father has hidden Easter gifts for all of us around the house and we have to find them all."

"Yes," said Cecil, "we have done very well we think, but we cannot find the last one. Can you help us?"

"I will try, boys," responded Holmes, "I trust you used my methods in finding the other gifts?"

"Oh yes" Arthur replied, "but now we don't even have a clue about the last one."

"Let's see if we can work this little problem out together. Have you any idea what this gift may be?"

Cecil said, "We think it's a book. Father buys us books often and none of the other gifts were books."

Holmes sat with his knees drawn up and his fingers steepled together, "I beg you not to speak to me for five minutes; it is quite a pretty problem you have presented me with." He sat there rigidly for five minutes, motionless with his eyes closed. Suddenly he leapt to his feet, "I have it," he cried, "it *is* a book, boys and I think the only safe hiding place would be in your father's study."

"But we have looked there, Mr Holmes."

"Ah, but how closely? I noticed a roll of tape in the hall as I entered and the tell tale signs of its recent usage on your father's hands. I suggest therefore that you will find the book, *'Golden Adventures for Children',* I suspect, taped to the underside of your father's desk."

The boys went off to hunt down their Easter treasure and the squeals of excitement we heard told us that once again Holmes had been proved right.

I looked across at a smiling Holmes, who was exchanging meaningful glances with Jacobs.

"Holmes, I do believe you cheated," I declared.

"Watson," he said, looking at Jacobs, "we also have our diplomatic secrets."

It is a fact that even whilst we are cocooned in this great city of ours, nature can make her presence felt. A gale shrieked and moaned outside on this particular day that I write of. I looked out of the window and was met with the sight of debris being picked up and hurled down Baker Street as though they were children's playthings. The windows rattled in their casement and the gas dimmed and lowered every few seconds. Holmes was busy continuing research he had undertaken into Early English Charters and appeared to be oblivious to the furious display of nature outside. As I crossed the room to pour myself another coffee, the wind shook the very fabric of the building so much, that it felt like we were in motion. Then, inexplicably, there was silence, followed by what seemed like an explosion. Everything inside the sitting-room that was not held down securely, jumped into the air.

"Good Heavens Holmes, what on earth was that?" I asked.

"I think, perhaps dear fellow, we should investigate and make sure no one outside has come to any harm."

The wind had died completely as had the normal street sounds we associated with this busy thoroughfare. We descended the seventeen steps, opened the front door to be met with quite an unbelievable sight. The house was surrounded by a great deal of what I thought were children, but then I recognised them as adults suffering from a form of Dwarfism. They were pointing at us and gesticulating wildly and peering at the very foundation of the house with looks of wonder and amazement. I feel I cannot do justice to what we observed, everything we now saw. The road, houses and indeed these little people were cloaked in the most vibrant hues; reds, oranges, yellows, greens. The surface of the road was a garish yellow and radiated out from a central point.

Holmes whispered to me, "Watson, I have a feeling we are not in Baker Street anymore."

Before I could answer we were approached by a most beautiful creature, who seemed somehow illuminated from within. She pointed at Holmes.

"My name is Glinda. Are you a good wizard or a bad wizard?" she asked of him.

Holmes took all this in his stride as though it was the most commonplace of dialogue, "I am not a Wizard of any kind, my name is Sherlock Holmes and this......"

"Oh well, is he the Wizard then " she asked, now turning her attention to me.

"I assure you, madam, that neither of us is a wizard, why on earth would you think such a thing?" Holmes asked her.

"The Munchkins called me and said a new wizard had just dropped a house on the Wicked Witch."

"Munchkins," I asked, "who or what are Munchkins?"

"Why, these are Munchkins," she answered, indicating the throng of little people surrounding us," and there is the Witch, under your house."

"My dear we owe you a thousand apologies, we had no intention of harming anyone."

"There is no need of an apology; the Munchkins have declared you both national heroes."

One of the little people, the Munchkins as she called them, stepped forward to me, "we'd like to thank you sweetly for doing it so neatly."

I stammered a reply and looked to Holmes, "how on earth do we get out of here, Holmes?"

"We will possess our souls in patience until we have gathered sufficient data to enable us to make good our return," he replied.

A piercing scream filled the air and an ugly looking witch, straight out of a child's story book descended on a broomstick. There were cries of, " Oh no, the Wicked Witch," all around.

I turned to Glinda, "Have we not destroyed the Wicked Witch?"

"This is her sister, and she's worse than the other one was."

"Who killed my sister? Was it you?" she screamed, fixing her eyes upon me.

"I assure you, madam, it was a complete and utter accident."

"Well," she said, looking even more threatening, "I can cause accidents too."

She walked over to all that was left of her sister, "where are the ruby slippers? Who has them? Give them back to me," she cried, working herself into a veritable frenzy.

"There they are," answered Glinda, pointing at me, "and there they will stay."

I looked down at my feet to find that instead of my normal footwear, my feet were now adorned with these ruby slippers; not a shade that best suits me it has to be said.

The Wicked Witch became hysterical at this point screaming over and over, "Give me back my slippers."

Holmes said to me, "Keep tight inside them, Watson, their magic must be very powerful or she would not want them so badly."

After issuing yet more threats of dreadful violence against our persons, she mounted her broomstick and was gone. Holmes took me to one side as the Munchkins continued their unrestrained celebrations.

"I am of the opinion, Watson that these slippers with the magic that is undoubtedly contained within them may hold the key to our safe return to dear old Baker Street." He stretched himself out on the ground and examined them for several minutes.

Glinda looked on, bemused, "Mr. Holmes, what are you looking for?"

"I am hopeful of using the magic powers of these slippers to return my friend and me back to our own life."

"Your friend has that power already."

"I do?"

"Those magic ruby slippers will take you home in two seconds. Now then, close your eyes and tap your heels together three times. Look at your friend and think to yourself, 'There's no place like home. There's no place like home.'

"There's no place like home, Holmes. There's no place like home, Holmes. There's no place like home, Holmes."

I awoke to find Holmes standing over me, with a smile on his face.

"My dear Watson, you are especially garrulous in your sleep today and surely only you could sleep with such a storm raging outside."

I stretched my limbs, got to my feet somewhat shakily and glanced out into the street. I was relieved to see normality, no Munchkins, no witches, just a resolutely ordinary Baker Street. Odd how the mind can play tricks on you like that whilst asleep.

"Watson?"

"Yes, Holmes?"

"Whatever have you got on your feet?"

When I glance over my copious notes and records of cases that Mr Sherlock Holmes has been involved in to some degree, I am faced by so many that are out of the commonplace and present so many singular, strange features that it is no easy matter for this humble chronicler to decide what narratives to lie before the public. The incident I am about to relate involved no known crime and the puzzle it presented to Holmes was one with no solution, yet it begs to be recalled as one of those whimsical moments that can occur at any time in a great city.

We both had broken our fast early for the heat was stifling and neither of us had felt able to sleep. The sunlight reflected off the buildings opposite, the light danced and filled the street and the early morning murmur of the city coming to life was now bursting into a symphony of noise, a paean to the rich, varied life that went on in London.

Holmes was busy reading *The Times* and I was attempting to write up the case of the Gondolier and the Russian Countess, when we heard footsteps ascending the stairs.

Holmes looked up, "Two men, Watson, one certainly taller and larger framed than the other, but even so as nimble and fleet of foot as his companion."

I had no time to reply before the door was flung open and two men such as described by Holmes entered the room. The larger of the two men, who towered over his companion addressed us, "Pardon me gentlemen for the intrusion, but we appear to be lost."

"Yes, that's right," said his companion, "and we don't know where we are either."

"You are in Baker Street," I answered.

"Baker Street where, sir?" asked the amply proportioned one.

"In London of course."

"London? London?? "He turned to his friend and said, "well, here's another nice mess you've gotten me into."

His response was to burst into tears, " I didn't mean to......I couldn't help it.....I just touched the button."

"You just can't leave anything alone can you? Pardon me, let me explain."

"Yes, please do," said Holmes, " beyond the obvious facts that you are both down on your luck, have both been in the US Navy, have bought a boat recently, have wives who hen-peck you and are regularly harassed by a balding Scotsman, I assure you I know nothing about you whatsoever."

"Does this guy know us, Ollie?"

"He most certainly does not and don't call me Ollie! Gentleman, my name is Hardy; Oliver Norvell Hardy and this is my friend Mr. Laurel."

"My name is Sherlock Holmes and this gentleman is Dr. Watson, now please explain to us the nature of your predicament"

"Well, it's like this, we were doing a spot of cleaning at the home of a scientist and he asked us not to touch a particular machine he was working on. Stan accidentally pressed one of the buttons, pulled four levers, turned three dials and engaged six of the gears and we found ourselves here in another country."

"I just wanted to know the time," said Mr Laurel.

"Then why did you have to interfere with that machine?"

"Well, he said it was a *time* machine, recomember? Say, did you say another country, Ollie? Is this London, England then?" asked Mr. Laurel.

"It certainly is," Mr. Hardy replied

"That's swell; I had an uncle once who was building a house in London, but he died."

"I am sorry to hear that Mr. Laurel, what did he die of?" I asked.

"A Tuesday.....or was it a Wednesday?" he said, looking most confused and ruffling his hair, which was standing up on end.

"No, my dear fellow, I meant what caused his death?"

"He fell through a trapdoor and broke his neck."

"Was he building his house at the time?" I further asked.

"No, they were hanging him," came the reply.

I looked across at Holmes and tried to get a silent message across that perhaps I should make an excuse to leave and send for the nearest constable as we were obviously in the presence of two escaped lunatics. To my surprise, far from being alarmed in their presence, he was laughing in that peculiar silent fashion of his; so much so, the very chair in which he was sitting was rocking back and forth.

"Well, gentlemen," Holmes said, his eyes twinkling merrily," I have some experience in the solving of puzzles and conundrums, but I fear this particular problem is beyond even my powers."

"Say, Ollie I have an idea."

126

Mr. Hardy's face bore a look of complete amazement at this remark from Mr. Laurel, "You do?"

"Sure, I'm not as dumb as you look."

"You certainly are not," answered Mr. Hardy, "well," he said, twiddling his tie, "we will leave you gentlemen in peace. Come, Stanley."

"Good-bye," shouted Mr. Laurel.

"Good day to you both," I said.

"Quick, Watson, we must run after them, not a moment is to be lost."

I was most gratified that Holmes had finally come to the same conclusion regarding our visitors as I had, "If we are to overcome them, should we not enlist the aid of the police, Holmes?"

"Overcome them, Watson? I have no intention of doing that."

"Then, why pray are we going after them?" I asked.

"Because my dear fellow, I have not laughed this much in a long time. Come, Watson."

My Coffee with Holmes (with nods to certain episodes of Frasier and Dad's Army)

I am afraid, Watson, that I shall have to go," said Holmes as we sat down to our breakfast together one morning.

"Go! Where to?"

"To the Langbourn Coffee House in Lombard Street."

I was not surprised. Indeed, my only wonder was that he had not already suggested such a visit. The Langbourn had been an occasional haunt of ours for some little time now, but now the extensive list of coffees available was greater still and it was the talk of London.

We had evidence of how popular the Langbourn had become when we went through its doors to the well planned and cosy interior. Every table was occupied.

"Busy," I said to Holmes.

"Well deduced, Watson," he said with a touch of asperity in his voice.

"There is a couple sitting by the window who appear to have finished their coffees, but show no signs of going."

"You mean the compositor from Shadwell who is discussing his lack of ambition with his second wife?" Holmes asked.

"Yes Holmes but how-?"

"You know my methods, Watson."

"I picked up the odd trick out in India and I believe I can give that couple the evil eye, causing them to shift somewhat more quickly than they might otherwise expect to."

"Let me see the look, Watson."

I shot Holmes a look of pure evil.

"No, I fear they will be there for a while yet my dear fellow."

128

"Shall we go ahead and order while we await a table?"

"What an excellent suggestion, Watson. I will have the Kenyan Super Blend."

I ordered a Jamaican blend which had caught my eye and at that moment a table became free and we seated ourselves.

"Would you mind if I asked you something Holmes?"

"Please do."

"Are you happy?"

There followed a few moments of silence where Holmes gazed into space.

"Did you hear the question Holmes?"

"Yes I am giving it some thought, it is a most singular and complex question."

"I do not believe so Holmes, either you are happy or you are not."

"I do have periods of great contentment, Watson and of satisfaction."

"Holmes, a straight answer if you please."

"My word Watson, is this the end of civilisation as we know it? Have the planets left their orbits? Look, brother Mycroft approaches."

I looked up and saw the portly figure of Mycroft Holmes threading his way through the tables with finesse I would hardly have given him credit for.

"Why, Sherlock and Doctor. I have not seen you in here before."

"Oh we come in from time to time you know, just to pass the time, but what brings you here?" said Holmes.

"Matters of high state, more than that I cannot say." With that he picked his way delicately through the tables once more and disappeared from view.

Just then our coffees appeared. Holmes addressed our waitress, "There is something floating on the surface of my coffee."

"Yes sir that is the cream."

"But I do not wish cream nor had I in fact requested it, could you please rectify for me?"

"Now then Holmes, that question once more. Are you happy?"

"Really Watson is it so important for you?"

"Can I not ask a simple question, Holmes?"

"Do you ask any other kind?" Holmes replied, laughing.

"Good morning, Mr Holmes and good morning to you too, Dr Watson." It was Inspector Lestrade looking more rat faced then ever if such a thing was possible.

"I cannot recall seeing the two of you in here before."

"Oh we come in from time to time you know, just to pass the time."

"Well I will not detain you, gentlemen. Good day to you."

The waitress bustled over to us once more. "Here you are sir; I hope this will be to your liking."

"What are the brown specks I can see?"Holmes asked.

"I dusted the coffee with cinnamon sir; it is a particular favourite of our more discerning clientele."

"Please take it away and bring exactly what I have ordered."

I took the opportunity to order another cup of the excellent Jamaican. The waitress beamed at me and scowled at Holmes and marched off.

"Everyone appears to be here this morning Holmes. Who next I wonder; Mrs Hudson?" said I chuckling.

"We must allow for all probabilities Watson, it has long been an axiom of mine."

My coffee was then delivered to me. Holmes looked at the waitress forlornly but she said, "don't worry sir; yours will be along soon enough. We have a team of specialists working on it right now."

Holmes harrumphed as only he can.

"Holmes, you still have not answered my question. Are you happy?"

"I am sorry my dear fellow, have I not answered that question?"

130

"You know full well you have not. You use the interruptions to prevaricate and procrastinate."

"Well if you must know, Watson...Ah, Mrs Hudson!"

"Hello gentlemen...I have not seen you in here before," that inestimable lady said.

"Oh we come in from time to.....oh never mind."

Mrs Hudson indicated a gentleman who accompanied her and introduced him as Arthur,"Arthur is a very good friend of mine gentlemen, but there is nothing in it. I don't want you to think anything else. We just keep other company occasionally."

"Of course, Mrs Hudson." I replied.

"What a pleasure to see Mrs Hudson so happy don't you think, Watson?"

"Yes indeed Holmes which brings me back to my evermore tedious original question. Are you happy?"

"If I could define happiness in any reasonable terms then I may be able to answer your question, but it remains an imponderable thing to me so I am not all sure I can answer your question in a way that would be entirely agreeable to you."

I nodded my head and realised I was not going to get a straight answer, "Forgive me Holmes, but I have to rush. I have arranged a game of billiards with Thurston and I do not like to keep him waiting."

"Yes of course my dear fellow, you get off."

Holmes remained sitting there for a while, tapping his fingers on the table in time with the clatter and chatter of ongoing conversations.

The waitress appeared once more and set down Holmes's coffee on the table with a thud that reverberated throughout the room.

"Kenyan Super Blend. No Cream. No cinnamon. Now, are you happy?"

"Do you know; in the grand scheme of things, yes I would say I am."

Sherlock Holmes vs Masterchef

Being a reprint from the reminiscences of John H Watson M.D

The day I took up residence at 221b Baker Street together with Mr Sherlock Holmes was a day that even at that early stage of our relationship served to illustrate how single minded a man my new friend was. Hardly had he finished dictating to me where my possessions should go and where my chair should reside, when he told me of a test he proposed to put to our landlady Mrs Hudson. He called that good lady to our sitting-room and outlined this test to her.

"What I want you to do, Mrs Hudson, is to prepare a three course meal for the good Doctor and me. This can be a meal of your choosing. This will be your chance to impress us."

"Mr Holmes, none of my previous tenants have had any complaints about the fare I produce for them," Mrs Hudson replied.

"Perhaps not, but maybe their standards were not as exacting as my own. It is four o' clock now. Shall we say six o' clock then? You have two hours, Mrs Hudson. Let's cook."

I thought that Holmes's manner with Mrs Hudson was brusque not to mention condescending and patronising and in spite of our friendship being new, I wasted no time in telling him so.

"We are", I said, "paying tenants and as such the good Mrs Hudson is our landlady not our servant."

"Exactly so and I have a mind to test what just what it is we pay our money for. If the food is not up to a certain standard then we may have to dine out a great deal."

"To be honest, Holmes, on my pension I fear dining out is beyond me."

"I do apologise for my thoughtlessness. I meant of course that *I* would have to dine out."

After a loud and I hoped telling harrumphing by me we adjourned to the kitchen to see what Mrs Hudson was producing for us. As befits Victorian gentleman we were totally unfamiliar with kitchens in general. I, for instance had not been in a kitchen since I was fifteen when our friendly cook or one of her 'girls' would give me occasional treats; of course that had nothing to do with *(Editor's note: Here the manuscript is faded and illegible. Rather than making wild and speculative guesses as to Watson's words here I have decided to leave a blank. The reader however is free to indulge in such guesses as they see fit).*

"What are you creating for us, Mrs Hudson?" asked Holmes.

"Kippers to start, gentlemen, on a bed of lettuce. Then braised pork with fried apples and a red wine reduction plus a medley of winter vegetables and to follow, bread and butter pudding."

"I fear you have left yourself a lot to do my dear lady. Are you confident you have the time to create this dish?" I asked.

"If not I think I will be like the fish I had yesterday."

"How do you mean?" asked Holmes.

"Gutted," she replied.

"Good luck. Dr Watson will bellow out in a strident manner at various intervals informing you how much cooking time you have left."

'Gutted', what a quaint expression I thought and made a mental note never to use it in polite company. When we were once more ensconced in the sitting-room Holmes asked for my views on the menu our landlady was favouring us with.

"Well I have to say that she may have bitten off more than she or possibly *we* can chew. There seems to be a tremendous amount of preparation to get through before she can even think of cooking the food itself."

"I agree, Watson and even though the food is fairly simple fare it is no easy matter to make those individual dishes work together. Fish

133

followed by the richness of pork and then the sticky sweetness of the bread and butter pudding. Cooking doesn't get any tougher than this. I really hope she can pull it all together."

"The bread and butter pudding I am really looking forward to, Holmes. I am very much a pudding person you know."

"Your shape rather gives credence to that statement, Watson. Well, we will possess our souls in patience for now."

When an hour had gone by I was dispatched by Holmes to announce to Mrs Hudson that she had one hour left. This I did in an *overly* strident manner causing a startled Mrs Hudson to drop a glass dish onto the floor. During the negotiations that followed I made the concession that I would sell my bull-pup to cover the cost of replacing said dish. When I was once again dispatched by Holmes on the thirty minute mark, I thought that discretion being the better part of valour; it would be as well on my part just to simply shout down the stairs. Some words of Mrs Hudson wafted back up to me; "stupid sausage neck" or something akin to that. Odd. I did not recall sausage being on the menu. It was a few minutes after six o'clock when Mrs Hudson set down her three plates of food before us.

"First of all, Mrs Hudson," Holmes said, "the dishes are nicely presented. Nevertheless, there are issues here. The kippers are off-centre giving the plate an untidy look, don't you think, Watson"

"The contents interest me much more than the appearance, can't we just eat the blessed meal?"

"Very well, Watson." Holmes lifted a forkful to his mouth, "The kippers are cooked to perfection. I commend you. The pork however could use a little more seasoning, but the overall effect is pleasing I must say."

"That pudding, Holmes. Now, that is sweet, sticky heaven. Mmm."

"Mrs Hudson, you have done very well. The balance of flavours was just right and you obviously know what you are doing. Mrs Hudson; I want to see you cook again. You may therefore cook for us on a daily basis."

The landlady, having been dismissed thus, walked to the door. As she opened it she looked back at Holmes, who now had his back to her, looking out the window. She raised her middle finger in an extraordinary upward motion and left the room. I was not altogether sure what this gesture meant, but I resolved never to ask her.

M

Yes that's right. Sherlock. Sherlock Holmes. You know the name I can see. In my opinion he is a busybody, a meddler and has been all his life. How dare he compare his brain to my vast intellect? You know where it comes from don't you, this enmity between us? Jealousy. He cannot bear to think there is someone with a brain inferior to his. He cannot take it I tell you. So I am misrepresented, showcased to the world as a mastermind, in charge of a huge organisation which exists purely for my benefit. He says as much to his friend Dr Watson, clothes me in a dramatic way to further his own ends, not mine mark you. He has a file on me which he thinks is complete, it is adorned with a giant 'M', if Watson so much as looks at the file then he is treated to another speech from that blessed man about me, he sneers he criticises. Jealousy, I tell you, jealousy. And now I feel the time has come to act, to break out of the mould he seems to have set for me. I have been incommoded long enough by the jibes and stung by the words. I have it all here in my notebook you see, the inconveniences I have been put to, all the times I have been hampered until I feel the restraint so hard upon me I must act and tonight I have. After slipping a certain little something into my overcoat pocket which I feel certain would bring these matters to a head, I set off with a certain amount of trepidation towards Baker Street.

If only you could see him the way I have to come to see him. His judgement on me clouded by pettiness and social inferiority. Yes I have seen him glance at the painting over my desk, not with admiration no but pure envy. No, you are wrong to argue the point; I know my man and what he feels for me. If he could bring me down he would, he knows it and I know it. I will not let him. Tonight was the night for bringing it all into the open.

Oh yes he was startled to see me. You should have seen the look on his face. Shock, horror and surprise. I slipped my hand into my overcoat pocket and he started. Oh yes, he started. He was not expecting such a bold move on my part. I withdrew the 'package'.

"A token Sherlock; to restoration of friendship. Merry Christmas."

"And Merry Christmas to you too, Mycroft."

I hardly cut a fine figure, running for the train as I was; coat flying everywhere as I sprinted the final few yards looking for the world as though I was attempting to become airborne in spite of the rather heavy holdall I was carrying or more accurately, dragging along in my wake. I made it with seconds to spare and set off in search of a seat. The train had older carriages with compartments and I was hoping for one all to myself, but on a Saturday morning it would be well nigh impossible I thought, but halfway down the sixth carriage, I found one. I almost missed it, in fact was three or four paces past it before I realised it, there followed some tricky manoeuvring as I tried to doge around a fellow passenger in the narrow corridor, but having extricated myself I entered the compartment and saw immediately that I was mistaken in my belief it was empty, for there was a youngish looking man, gazing out of the window. I gave him a cheery greeting which rather belied how I was feeling, hoisted my bulging holdall onto the luggage rack and settled down. I sat down opposite my travelling companion and gave him a cursory examination, youngish was the best I could come up with age-wise, short blond hair, a very distinctive nose and balanced on it precariously a pair of horn rimmed glasses; he returned my glance momentarily before resuming his scenery watching.

"A fine day for travelling," I ventured.

"Yes it is," he replied and once again returned his gaze to the window.

We were hurtling through the Wiltshire countryside; I had joined the train at Salisbury and was en route for the town of Lyme Regis, an idyllic town, almost picture-book in its loveliness.

I was going to the wedding of an old friend of mine, John Ransome, who was now taking the plunge at the age of forty-five. I had long ago become convinced that he was a confirmed bachelor and would remain so but it seems Cupid had fired its dart and found its target once more. I had seen very little of him of late and indeed still had to meet his bride so I was more than pleased to receive his invitation; the ceremony was to be held in St Michaels Church and the reception in a local hotel, The Royal Lion.

"It's a lovely part of the world isn't it?" I said.

"Yes, I used to travel through it often a long time ago".

"Me too," I replied, "First time for a few years now."

"And where are you bound for if you don't mind me asking?"

"Lyme Regis, I am going to a wedding there today."

"Not John Ransome's wedding?"

"Well, yes....you too?"

"Yes, my name is James Burt; I was at University with John."

I had no real reason to doubt the veracity of that statement, yet he seemed far too young to have been at University the same time as John, but it hardly seemed appropriate for me to question him on it so I just let it go.

"When did you last see him?" I asked, being by now, very curious, "by the way my name is Gary Middleton."

"Oh, it's been a long time. We lost touch many, many years ago."

"Lucky he managed to track you down then so he could get a invitation to you."

"Ah, well if it comes to that, I haven't got an invitation as such, but I heard about the wedding and long, long ago when we were close we promised each other that whatever happened, wherever we were, we would attend each other's wedding, so here I am, promises must be kept don't you think ?"

"I am sure he will be surprised to see you and there is bound to be a spare bed at the hotel you can purloin, did John attend your wedding or.........?"

"No, I never married," he replied.

We travelled the rest of the way in virtual silence. I buried myself in the newspaper and he once again studying the fields and hills as they rushed past. I realised we were now very close to Axminster and walked into the corridor to stretch my legs and to use the toilet. When I returned there was no sign of my companion, probably gone to stretch his legs too and wait by the door I thought. I saw no sign of him on the platform either but thought little of it. The bus to Lyme was outside and I clambered on, mentally urging my erstwhile companion to hurry up and board, but there was no sign of him.

After freshening up at The Royal Lion, I had a quick sandwich and pint in the bar and then ambled down Broad Street towards the church. Although I was of the opinion I was far too early, there were a few people gathered there. I spotted John and walked on up to him, smiles on both our faces.

"How are you, John?"

"Happy, Gary, very happy," he laughed, "so good to see you, glad so many of my old friends could make it."

"I actually met one of your old mates on the train, John."

"Really? Who was that then?........oh no.....sorry Gary, I see Great Aunt Edith approaching.....er....must dash, we'll have a long chat later."

I exchanged pleasantries with a whole range of people, none of whom I knew in the slightest and one by one we headed into the church. The bride, Suzanne, looked truly radiant, only matched by Johns' smile when he caught sight of her. The service passed off without a hitch, but immediately after being declared husband and wife, they both turned round to face the congregation with the broadest of smiles when something happened which chilled everyone there. John was letting his eyes wander all over the church, nodding at folk when he suddenly had a look of abject horror on his face, he half pointed at something or someone and with his face deathly white and his whole body swaying, he collapsed at the feet of his family. While everyone's attention was on John I looked towards the back of the church to see, what, if anything, could have caused John to react like that. Standing by the door, I could see James, my fellow passenger of the morning, but would the shock of seeing his old friend have caused such a violent reaction and that look of horror?   John came to his senses but looked shaky and after a lengthy interval, we were back on schedule with the photographer doing his thing. During the setting up of one of the shots, I managed to have a word with John as he was talking to his mother.

"Are you ok, John, what happened?"

"Been trying to explain it to Mum, but it was the oddest thing, as I looked around at all the family and friends, I could have sworn I saw my old friend, James Burt, standing large as life by the door and then I remembered the promise we had made each other to attend each other's wedding and the next thing I knew I was in a heap on the floor"

"But you did see him, John"

141

"W-W-What, you saw him too?"

"Yes I tried to tell you earlier, he was on the train with me, he told me about the promise."

John again looked ready to fall, his lips moved but no words came, his mother moved closer to me and leant her head towards mine.

"Gary.......James Burt died over twenty years ago."

I was now lost for words and the only thing I could think to say was:

"Well, a promise *is* a promise."

Christmas was nearly over; over as soon it had begun almost. The house was still full however of assorted Uncles and Aunties and rarely seen cousins, and they showed no signs of going. Gary, being the only teenager present, was about as bored as he could be and quietly slipped out the back door.

The neighbourhood of Lyme Regis was still very new to him as he and his parents had only been here a few short weeks, so he thought a little exploration may relieve the boredom. Not far from home there was a leafy lane; Haye Lane, which appeared to lead nowhere in particular, but new as he was, he had picked up the local gossip from the kids at Woodroffe School about a haunted house at the end of this lane and the thought of giving it the once over both thrilled and scared him.

He ambled down the lane, kicking piles of leaves into the hedge as he went. It seemed to go on forever, but after a few minutes he found himself standing by a pair of rusty wrought-iron gates. He pushed them open and made his way across the overgrown garden, through which he could see the house; an unremarkable grey stone building, not your classic haunted house look at all. He peered through the glass on the front door; it certainly looked empty although he had heard there was some sort of caretaker who looked in from time to time. He just had to go in now he had got this far and if he should happen to come across anyone, could explain himself away easily enough.....new kid in town....got lost etc. No big deal.

143

The sky had darkened and the first drops of rain began to fall, that made up his mind for him.....he tried the door handle, it turned easily and the door slid open, he was pleased at this, at least the crime of breaking and entering could not be added to trespass if things went wrong. There were a few sticks of furniture around, but little else other than cobwebs. This caretaker could not be earning his money with his cleaning skills he thought, that's for sure. Now he was in here, he was disappointed, it was just an old empty house, neither exciting nor scary. He tried the upstairs rooms, all perfectly empty and lifeless. Outside a storm was raging, thunder rolling around and the interior of the house was being illuminated by lightning flashes. The rain was hammering on the roof and windows, now. Gary might not have been scared by the house, but he sure as hell was not going out in that weather. He descended the stairs and as the lightning flashed he could see a man standing at the bottom. Oops found out.

"Sorry mister, I was out walking and got caught in the storm and ran in here to get dry," he thought he sounded convincing.

The man, an old man, took some time mulling this over and seemed to accept it, "it's ok kid, no harm done," he said.

"You must be the caretaker," Gary said.

"That would be me; I flit in from time to time, just to keep an eye on things. You must be new around here; local kids tend to keep away".

"Yeah, we have just moved into Blue Waters Drive. I heard this dump was haunted or something."

"And you, kid, you're not scared?"

Even if he was, Gary was not about to admit it.

"If it's a ghost story you're looking for, I can help you there, come in the drawing room with me, we'll light a couple of candles and I'll tell you about it".

Gary hesitated and almost unknowingly took a step backwards.

"So you are scared, kid," the caretaker mocked.

"No, mister, not me," said Gary, his bravado returning.

They settled themselves into two old dusty armchairs and as the storm raged outside, the old man started his tale.

"Long time ago, this house was owned by two sisters, both elderly and both spinsters. They had virtually no family save for the odd nieces and nephews scattered all over the country. One of the nieces, Emily Wade, came here for an extended holiday and met a local guy, John Burnham. They saw a lot of each other during the time she was here but all too soon, the visit was over and she headed back to Rochester in Kent. They wrote to each other and vowed undying love, and counted down the days until they could see each other again, which would be on her next visit".

"Excuse me, but why didn't this Burnham guy go to Kent to see her?"

"Pressures of work kept him in Lyme, he was very single-minded and despite his words of love to Emily, he was happy to be patient, knowing she was his. In time of course, she came back and they took up where they had left off. She was all for marriage but he was fighting shy of the idea and kept her hanging on. Inevitably it all cooled down between them, she was tired of waiting whereas he was happy enough to throw himself into his work knowing she was always there for him. She wanted to break off this so-called 'engagement' but he was adamant he would not let her go, she was his.

145

A few weeks passed during which they hardly saw anything of each other and one fateful week, Burnham had to travel up country to attend a funeral of a family member. He was going to be gone for seven days at least. This was an immense relief to Emily who no longer had to fear; at least for a week, his unannounced visits and unknown to Burnham she had another admirer, who would be just as happy to see the back of him for a week. You can imagine what happened, Burnham came back early and caught Emily and her lover together; in the room above us actually, kid"

"What happened?" Gary was well and truly hooked now.

"Simple, kid, he murdered her".

"And the lover?"

"The lover was never seen again, kid. The police put two and two together and decided that the lover was also the killer hence his disappearing act. No one had seen Burnham return to the area, so he upped and quietly left and re-appeared two days later to be met with the awful news about Emily"

"So then, it's Emily's ghost that haunts this house," Gary said.

"No you smart-ass kid, no its not. Emily has never been seen or heard since, in this house or anywhere. But.... oddly enough, John Burnham also died in this house, upstairs in Emily's old room. By this time, the two spinster sisters had also died and the house was empty. Burnham had an incurable disease and came here to die....by his own hand, and that, kid, is that".

Outside the storm was still continuing; the wind was shrieking and the rain falling steadily.

"But it's not even a ghost story and you promised me a ghost story. It's not even a very good murder story mister; it doesn't make sense for one thing".

"In what way?" asked the caretaker.

"If the police thought the lover killed Emily and this Burnham had some sort of alibi, like not being in the area, how come you know so much about it, how come you know he killed Emily?"

"That's easy, kid. I *am* John Burnham."

Swish

The street was quiet. Coombe Street always was at this time of day. Very quiet. Eerily quiet you could say, but he was a God fearing upright man and thoughts such as these did not bother him. His own footsteps echoed in the narrow street. Even his measured tread proclaimed his steadfastness. But, wait. What was that? Another sound reached his ears.

Swish....swish....swish.

He turned and looked down the empty street. Nothing. And so, nothing to fear. On he walked, but still the sound persisted.

Swish...swish....swish.

A woman's dress maybe? At this early hour? Surely not. A cloak such as a footpad might attire himself in? But he had never heard of such violence in the town. A priest's robes? He hoped that would be the case. He was the most righteous of men and he would warmly accept the comradeship of a priest at this hour, this black hour. But, whether a priest or not, why did he not show himself? How could he remain hidden?

As soon as he began to walk again, the noise resumed.

Swish...swish....swish.

But surely closer now. Louder, certainly. He recited the words of a prayer to himself, repeating the words over and over. Terror washed over him. Even though he could not see the begetter of these sounds he knew for sure that the face would be lifeless and formless. In his mind's eye he could see the blankness of the face. The certain knowledge that it would have no eyes, no nose, no mouth. Just a void. The words of more prayers came to him in this, his hour of need. The sound was almost unbearable now, it seemed to be all around him, enveloping him like a black mass and pulling him down with its evil. Yes it was evil, he knew that. He did not know why he, a devout and pious man should be singled out for the attention of this malevolent being. He covered his ears with his hands and cried out to be saved. He collapsed into a doorway and lay prostrate making the sign of the cross over and over. A touch on his shoulder brought him rapidly to his feet, heart pounding.

A priest! It was a priest after all!! How foolish he now seemed. He was helped to his feet by the kindly priest.

"You must forgive me, Father. You must think me a madman."

"I can see you have had a shock of some kind, my son."

"A shock brought on by my own foolishness, Father."

As they walked on together he relayed to the priest how he had spooked himself and how relieved he was to be now in the company of a devout man like himself. He didn't seem to notice now the swish...swish...swish of the priest's robes. It held no terror for him now as it did only a short few minutes before.

"I am a virtuous and Godly man, Father. If such things as wicked spirits could have a hold over me then life would truly not be fair."

"It isn't," replied the priest, his oddly unformed face now turned in his direction.

Visitors

Sad.

Sad that houses such as this were no longer lived in. Their glorious histories blunted by the endless stream of visitors, who admire, but don't cherish, who show astonishment, but no affection. Where once had been life, there now was sterility. The constant stream of footsteps now reverberated thorough out the house, where formerly there had been animated conversations, love matches, intrigues, and the sounds of children playing. If only these walls could speak, what tales they could tell.

She liked to come here at quiet times when the tourists found themselves other destinations to trample over. Alone with her thoughts, she wandered over the house. In the vast dining room, she pictured in her mind's eye a great banquet underway; the butler with his liveried staff waiting to serve the family and guests from a mouth watering array of dishes. The polite conversation, the gossip, the social niceties as the clicking of the waiters heels counted down the time. She could not help but smile at these images which danced and flickered in her mind.

From there to the library. The smell of the bound volumes adorning its shelves hit her first as it always did. She inhaled deeply and let the tales of ages consume her. These books, these wondrous books were alive, did not the visitors realise that? They spoke to her. They whispered to her. They reached out to her. And now, the men folk, cigar in one hand, a glass of port in the other, restraints of the day forgotten, would stretch out in the exquisitely upholstered chairs.

Mostly in silence they would sit, occasionally a burst of conversation would arise only to be swallowed up by the crackling of the fire. She would not, could not share these quixotic images with the visitors whose only concern was to look the house over, nod appreciably then head to the gift shop for postcards to send to loved ones. They missed the beating of the heart of this place, it cried out to be loved again.

Sad.

Sad she felt as she entered the ballroom. Those dances of yesteryear, such fine occasions, were no more. Piped music came out of unsympathetically designed and placed speakers, at such a quiet volume so as not to irritate the tourists. Balls were once held here that were the envy of the whole county. People would come from miles around to take part. The finest musicians would be down from London and would exhaust the dancers long before they themselves felt any fatigue. Now this grand ballroom was empty, its stripped wooden floor would no longer echo to the sounds of a hundred pairs of feet dancing gaily. Lining the room were glass display cabinets which housed the silver of families now long gone. More like prisoners, the beautiful silver plates, chalices were locked away like shameful objects, to be stared at from a distance lest they taint those who come into contact with them. Reflected in the one of the plates she caught a movement of a figure behind her. So be it, even at quiet times she could not expect to have the room to herself. She felt it incumbent on her to at least be civil, she turned to speak, but she was alone. Odd. She could have sworn a figure was there. Perhaps they had moved through quickly to the ante-room, not wishing to disturb her.

How she wished she could handle these precious objects, to run her hands over their smooth surfaces. Hold on. There's that reflection again. She only half-turned before she realised there was someone standing right by her. She must have been so engrossed she had not heard his approach.

"I am sorry, did I startle you?" he said in a warm, honeyed and soothing voice.

"No, not really. If anything I startled myself."

"Yes, I could see your thoughts were elsewhere."

Yes, she agreed and then moved on. She had been polite, but she needed her solitude when she came here. She could allow no distractions. She loved everything about this house, it was just such a shame she could not have it all to herself. She walked down the Gallery, a long corridor which ran the whole length of the east wing. She knew every nuance of every painting which hung there; they were old friends to her. She stopped dead. There in front of a few paces away was the man she had encountered in the ballroom, but how on earth had he got ahead of her. Yes, she had been absorbed in her thoughts, but even so she thought she would have noticed him walk past.

"You look at those paintings with so much love in your eyes," he said.

"I do love them, that is why," she said.

As she answered him, she realised she could see that self same love in his eyes too. His was an almost reverential look.

"As do I. I always have, for a long, long time," he replied.

"Please excuse me, but you don't seem like the normal tourist I am used to seeing here."

He laughed," I was about to say the same thing to you. I think you love this house every bit as much as I do."

"Yes I do, I can never keep away for long."

"I feel the same," he said, "I am here quite often, the house sort of calls to me."

"Have you some sort of connection to the house then?" she asked.

"On many levels, but chiefly because I was born here," he answered, "and you? Have you a connection; you're not going to tell me you were born here too are you?"

"Oh no," she said, "I *died* here."

Surprise

The inquest, the police investigation and what a joke that was, were now over. All he wanted was a return to normality. The new, perceived normality that was going to be his. No more questions, no more pointing fingers in the street, but who was he kidding? The questions that he had endured would always be asked, but silently, in the shadows. Well, let them wonder, let them surmise. He was an innocent man. Death by accident was the verdict and it would stay that way, a testimony to his innocence.

The questions still rang in his mind. 'You say you put your arm around Mr Taylor at the top of the stairs?' 'Yes.' 'Do you consider that this would in any way account for his losing his footing?' 'No, not at all, the contact was minimal.' 'But, maybe if he was taken by surprise?' 'No, we very often came down the stairs that way.' 'So you maintain that this action of yours would not have resulted in Mr Taylor losing his balance, there was, for instance, no forward pressure applied, however slight?' 'Absolutely not, he must have tripped, as he began to fall I reached out for him, but his sleeve slipped through my grasp.'

On and on it went, just like poor Maurice himself, down that long staircase. Eventually, the verdict was returned and he went back to the house that was now his, to quiet, peace and solitude. Oh yes, he thought, there would have to be changes. Maurice hated change, but now he was no longer around he could start to have things his way, the pictures on the walls re-arranged, those hideous ornaments which Maurice collected can now be consigned to the bin. As he thought this, one of those self-same ornaments detached itself from its display

154

position and crashed to the floor. He was not a man easily spooked and saw it for what it was; an unsafe shelf which would now be replaced.

Yet he was not entirely without compassion and feeling. How different it had been in the early years. Everything was new and fresh. How they laughed. Maurice was forever creeping up behind him...and digging his fingers in below his ribs and shouting 'Surprise!' Playful, yet intense because of the love that lay behind it. 'Surprise'; it never failed to make him smile. How that was to change as the years went by. God, how he hated Maurice coming up behind him, 'Please don't say it, please don't say it'. Useless and redundant thoughts because he always said it, year after bloody year. Couldn't the man tell how much he hated it, how had he grown so insensitive? Oh well, Maurice was gone now and he was here. And life, as he said to himself was for the living.

He walked around his new kingdom, making notes of where to make changes, what to put where, what to throw out, what to keep. Although tired, the idea that came to him infused him with a great energy and it was 1am before he admitted defeat and headed off to bed. His sleep was fitful and his dreams when they came were nightmarish landscapes, full of blackness and black deeds. As he awoke from one of these, he could have sworn he heard footsteps outside his room. The dream had made him shaky most likely, but no, there it was again. Peering into the gloom outside of his room he could see nothing. He momentarily thought to himself that he had never quite encountered darkness as impenetrable as this. And the silence. The silence had the whole of history caught up in it. A silence that could never be broken.

Was that a movement at the bottom of the stairs? A slight impression of a fleeting shadow. He looked down from the top step. No, nothing caught his eye. All was quiet; all was dark, so very dark. And then.....two sudden points of pressure on his body. A slight, almost imperceptible push. As he cart wheeled down the long, long staircase toward oblivion, a single word broke the silence:

'Surprise.'

\

Was he dead? Was he dreaming? He felt distant from himself almost as though he were floating high on the ceiling and looking down on his own faltering progress down this endless corridor. Perhaps he was dead and this is how it feels as the spirit leaves the body. His footsteps echoed on the flagstones although he could not feel the impact of his feet on them. Was he then in limbo? How could he not know what state he was in? The thought terrified him, the thought he was not in control. He prided himself on his mastery of any situation he found himself, but the dripping and cold stone walls gave him no comfort, no answers. He was in the Castle Lochan, he knew that much. At the request of his old school friend from forty years ago; Fitzroy, now the Laird of Lochan. He was surprised to get such an invitation from one he never really knew that well and one he had not set eyes on for well over thirty years. It had puzzled him that Fitzroy appeared to employ no servants or if he did so they were unheard and unseen. The evening meal had been exquisite and the wine flowed freely. What was it he was trying to remember? Something important. Something which had unsettled him. Think he told himself, think! Yes, Fitzroy! He had scarcely seemed to age at all, the lines so prominent on his own face were not reflected in his host's features. And why had Fitzroy not eaten? Think. Remember! A curious digestion problem that was it, that was the explanation offered. But why think of that now? All he wanted to do was wake up from this dream if indeed it was a dream. Now he found himself in the library with its dusty volumes unloved and uncared for. But how? He had not opened the door. My God was he dead after all? Had he floated through the solid wall as though he were not there? And yet, and yet his conscious mind was still reasoning, still searching for answers, would that be the case if he were really dead? Was there a purpose to this nocturnal wandering?

Was he being drawn to something? His ultimate destination, his goal? On he wandered; doors that were closed to him neither slowed him down nor barred his progress. He could see a light, perhaps the warmth of a blazing fire to assuage his morbid feelings and lift his heart. Or was it Heaven he could see? This was the final journey of his miserable soul. Something imprinted itself on his brain. Fitzroy did drink wine last night although he had not partaken of any other sustenance. But what did that mean? Why did it seem to matter? He drank out of his own bottle, yes, that was odd and though he was the perfect host he had not offered any of that remarkably rich red wine to his guest. Shivers wracked his body. Cold? Fear? Fear of death unless of course he was dead. The light he could see was closer; it was a fire in a room he had not been shown when receiving his guided tour yesterday. In front of this welcoming fire was Fitzroy, Laird of Lochan, in full Highland regalia complete with a ceremonial sword, his eyes blazing red like the fire itself. He could feel no warmth, his body remained icy cold, like a statue he thought.

"Fitzroy....am I dead?"

The air whistled as the blade came forward tearing skin on impact.

"You are *now*."

Lyme first entered recorded history in 774AD when King Cynewulf of the West Saxons granted land on the west bank of the River Lym not far from its mouth, to the monks of Sherborne Abbey for the production of sea-salt. There is no reason to suppose that salt boiling had not gone for many, many years before that. Salt production and fishing would have been the chief occupation of anyone living in the small community. Lyme, from the start was dependant on the sea, in fact, without it, Lyme would never have existed.

In 833AD there occurred one of those incidents which became part and parcel of the history of the area. The Danes who were a constant menace and having met with repulses at other parts of the coast, set sail for Charmouth where they wrought great havoc and slaughter. King Egbert gathered up as large an army as he could muster and met the Danes in battle. The numbers of the Danes may well have been bolstered by the rebellious Cornish Britons as was indeed the case during the reign of King Athelstan some time later. Egbert nearly won the day, but for the steady supply of fresh men coming ashore from the Danish ships (some thirty five in total with maybe around fifteen thousand men at their disposal). The Saxons were routed although the Danes decided against forming a community at Charmouth, perhaps fearing another attack from Egbert.

From the great Domesday Book of 1086 we can glean a little of life in Lyme at that time. There is an entry recording Lyme as having twenty seven salt workers who paid a shilling each and the fishermen of Lyme paid fifteen shillings to the monks for the privilege of fishing here.

In 1145 a Papal Bull signed by Pope Eugenius III confirmed that Lyme and its fishing rights belonged to the Abbey of Sherborne. Lyme had become a town of some prosperity by the reign of Henry III and was chosen by Henry to be the port from where Queen Eleanor and Prince Edward would depart for Gascony in 1254. To that end, Gilberts of London, acting for the King, instructed the Bailiffs of Lyme to impress ships for this purpose. In 1271 Lyme was also given the right to hold a weekly market and a fair. There was often some tension in the town owing to a feud with the sailors from Dartmouth in Devon; no doubt a result of trade differences. This trouble went as far as murder and Henry III had to intervene and decreed that the sheriffs of the two counties should summon witnesses to an inquisition and ascertain who the guilty parties were and arrest those responsible. History remains quiet thereafter on this particular quarrel although tensions remained between the two towns for some considerable time.

Changes came quickly during the reign of Edward I. Around the eighth year of his reign (c.1280) the manor of Lyme that was formerly belonging to Sherborne Abbey now became Crown property, this was true of the lands around Lyme belonging to Glastonbury Abbey also. Lyme, having now become the King's demesne it now carried the suffix 'Regis'; King's Lyme. Edward granted the town its first Royal charter in 1284, this being expanded at the beginning of 1285 (and thereafter renewed and refined by various monarchs). The granting of such a charter may seem to confer a special status upon Lyme, but the truth was that it was more to do with policy and increasing the revenue due to the crown. Edward was fairly liberal when it came to the granting of Royal charters; in 1284 alone seven other towns were granted the same status. There were advantages to the town certainly; trading privileges were now considerably enhanced bringing increased prosperity. Although under the keen eyes of the King's Bailiff and therefore the crown itself, there was some degree of self government. It also meant Lyme now had the right to send two members to Parliament; in spite of the town's somewhat turbulent political history this remained the state of affairs from 1295 until 1832 when only one member was returned and finally in 1868 Lyme lost its voice in Parliament. This first charter also gave Lyme the right to a merchant guild reinforcing the view that there must have been considerable trading already going on. It is known that Lyme exported wool to France in exchange for wine as early as 1157. It may be a fair assumption then that the Cobb existed at that time in one form or another. The first mention proper of the Cobb occurs in 1294; it would have been formed by driving wooden piles to the sea bed (oak being preferred) and large boulders as a kind of infill. In spite of the protection it offered to the trade and therefore prosperity of the town, it was not infallible as a barrier against the severest of storms. Many times the town had to go cap in hand to the reigning monarch begging for both a reduction of the current tax burden and for funds to repair the Cobb, harbour and dwellings.

In 1347 Lyme supplied four ships and sixty two mariners to assist at the siege of Calais. The town then became prone to attacks from the French ostensibly in the furtherance of The One Hundred Years War between England and France, but often through private raiding parties. Lyme was still in fear of these attacks from privateers for many years to come.

Further destructive attacks came not from the French, but from the sea itself. In the 1370's the Cobb was destroyed by a major storm as it had been in 1340; this particular tempest was very severe taking with it upwards of eighty houses and nigh on forty boats being lost. This was a scenario to be repeated often in varying degrees. In 1481 for instance, the Burgesses of Lyme petitioned King Edward IV for help because the town had been wasted by the tides and the overflowing of the sea causing many inhabitants to depart, the port having been by tempest destroyed. Part of the tax burden on Lyme was relaxed for sixty five years as a result of this petition.

In Elizabethan times trade had reached its summit; there was a new found wealth in the town, merchants prospered with trading links reaching out to Africa, the West Indies and the Americas. Apprehensive eyes looked out to see for the next threat; the Spanish! As it became clear an invasion was imminent the ship builders of Lyme were instructed to fit out two ships to help combat the coming Armada. These were the 'Jacob' and the 'Revenge' although the Spanish fleet passed on by in the end. An idea of the spirit of the town (the 'heretic' town according to Queen Mary in 1558 who had stopped an annual grant of £20 to help maintain the Cobb) can be gained by the fact that the burgesses of the town seemed to be more preoccupied with the failure of towns such as Axminster and Taunton to come up with their share of the Armada levy; the letters to the Privy Council from the town are full of outrage at their having to, in their eyes, foot too much of the bill. For the next fifty years or so the town continued to prosper, enjoying also a period of relative peace and calm. The Civil War brought this period to a shattering conclusion.

The Royalist cause was being hampered by its inability to control the sea; the advantages in taking Lyme were all too apparent (in a maritime survey of 1589 Lyme was adjudged to be the third largest port in England) and King Charles accordingly instructed Sir John Stawell, Governor of Taunton to raise a force to march against 'ye rebellious town of Lyme' and assist in its submission. The Royalist forces, numbering around six thousand, were commanded by Prince Maurice of the Rhine. Their headquarters were established at Haye House with the army being camped around the area of Colway Manor. The siege began in earnest in April 1644 against a garrison of perhaps five hundred men in Lyme aided and abetted ably by the men and women of the town. The defences held firm in spite of the superior forces stacked against them. The Royalist forces were unable to take control of the Cobb or establish any kind of blockade which meant that supplies for the town were able to get through; food, ammunition and men. Time was not on

Prince Maurice's side and the King more or less spelt out to him in a letter that as the siege was going nowhere his troops would be better deployed elsewhere. Despite this Maurice kept the siege going for another month before eventually admitting defeat and withdrawing. The losses amongst the Royalists were put at two thousand to three thousand, but this seems unfeasibly high; the casualty figures as recorded were seemingly higher than those they suffered at Exeter or Bristol. The losses in the town amounted to one hundred and twenty, but the damage to the buildings of Lyme was severe.

Another period of calm ensued during which the Commonwealth government agreed funds to modernise the Cobb and harbour. The Cobb was extended and existing walls extended to allow larger ships to use the harbour. During the next four decades trade continued as before and Lyme again knew peace.

The town was once more plunged into turmoil when the Duke of Monmouth, who had been in exile in Holland, returned to this country where he was planning a Protestant revolt against his uncle, the Catholic King James II. Lyme had been picked out by the Duke's mother, no doubt for its well known Protestant sympathies. Several of the townspeople joined his small army and more flocked down to Lyme to join when the news of his arrival spread. The enterprise was doomed to failure from the start and the rebels were routed at the battle of Sedgemoor and Monmouth captured. Monmouth's execution on Tower Hill was botched, but still humane compared with the end of some of those who supported him. Twelve local men were sentenced by Judge Jeffreys to be hung, drawn and quartered. The grisly fate that met these men was meted out on the very spot where Monmouth had disembarked.

For some time after the Monmouth rebellion Lyme continued to be a busy port and trade flourished with ships setting out from Lyme for far distant ports, but ironically it was this flourishing international trade that was to be Lyme's downfall. The new trade routes demanded bigger and better vessels and the port of Lyme was too small to accommodate these bigger vessels and when coupled with the rise of industries in the north, it spelled ruin for Lyme Regis. Late on in the 18th century the population had dropped from a peak of three thousand to a little over a thousand. As the road network in England advanced it meant that many more goods could now be carried by road. By 1750 the town was in a parlous state; buildings were left empty when families moved to pastures new. Lyme was dead on its feet and still cut off to some extent from the outside world. Almost unbelievably, it was as late as 1759 before wheeled traffic could get down the long hill into Lyme. Previously it had been the preserve of hardy men and even hardier packhorses to climb in and out of Lyme on well defined, but hardly comfortable tracks to meet the old Roman road (now the route of the A35).

Just as the sea had been a frequent enemy to the town as well as a begetter of bounties, so it now came to the rescue. The early to mid 18th century had begun to see a rise in the taking of sea water for one's health; not just for bathing in, but drinking also. Lyme, in common with many towns on the south coast was slower to embrace this new life afforded them because the threat from privateers was still ever present and as we have seen the non-existence of a route for wheeled traffic would have rendered any idea of Lyme turning into a fashionable resort laughable. The creation of the new road began to change that, but perhaps the greatest fillip accorded the town was the philanthropic nature of Thomas Hollis of Corscombe who dedicated the last few years of his life to enhancing Lyme's outlook and reputation. Buildings were bought and then demolished to unclutter the lower part of town; he purchased land by the shore to enable the creation of a new walkway, purely for pleasure, known as 'The Walk' (now Marine Parade) and Hollis set the wheels in motion for Lyme to have its own Assembly Rooms. He did not live to see his plans come to final fruition; the Rooms being completed in 1775 the year after his death. The rooms quickly became the centre for the town's fashionable society.

More storms in 1792 and 1817 necessitated further extensive repairs to the Cobb. These repairs were carried out by the Royal Engineers led by Captain D'Arcy in 1795 and Colonel Fanshaw in 1818. A further great storm of 1824 brought the Royal Engineers into action once again; this time most of the Cobb was rebuilt and clad with the Portland stone that is seen today.

1799 was a momentous year for Lyme Regis for it saw the birth of Mary Anning in May. Mary Anning was born into a humble family of dissenters. She and her brother Joseph were the only survivors among 10 children born to Richard Anning and his wife Mary Moore. Her father Richard was a carpenter and cabinet-maker who taught his daughter how to look for and to clean fossils. They sold the 'curiosities' they collected from a stall on the seafront, where they found customers among the middle classes who flocked to Lyme in the summer. In 1811, Mary's brother Joseph found a skull protruding from a cliff. Over a period of months Mary painstakingly uncovered an almost complete skeleton of a 'crocodile'. The specimen was bought by the local lord of the manor Henry Hoste Henley who sold it to William Bullock for his Museum of Natural Curiosities in London. This brought Mary's reputation to the attention of scientific circles. The specimen was later named *Ichthyosaurus*, the 'fish-lizard', by scientists de la Beche and Conybeare. Mary died from breast cancer, aged 47. For one with such disadvantaged beginnings, she had gained the respect and imagination of the scientific establishment who gave her recognition in her lifetime. Nine years before her death she was given an annuity, or annual payment, raised by members of the British Association for the Advancement of Science and the Geological Society of London. She was the first honorary member of the new Dorset County Museum. Her death in 1847 was recorded by the Geological Society (which did not admit women until 1904) and her life commemorated by a stained glass window in St Michael's Parish church in Lyme.

In 1803, ironically on the 5th of November, a fire started that destroyed forty two houses in the Coombe Street and Mill Green area. 1803 was also the year of Jane Austen's first visit to Lyme; in fact she was in the town as late as November and witnessed the great fire as she mentioned in a letter some five years later. Jane, together with some of her family returned the following year, this time in the summer, for a few weeks. They were believed to have lodged in Pyne House in Broad Street, but after some of the party had moved on to Weymouth and beyond, cheaper lodging were sought. No one can be certain where they stayed, but evidence in Jane's letters point to a boarding house not too far from Pyne House, possibly Hiscotts (now the site of the sadly empty Three Cups hotel). Jane Austen's last great novel 'Persuasion', is in part, set in Lyme Regis. The crucial passage set in Lyme is the central link in the story which begins in the Somerset countryside and moves to its climax in Bath. Jane Austen's settings for her novels were not usually real places: Lyme is one of the few exceptions, together with Bath. Persuasion was published posthumously in 1818, and the town has been a centre of literary pilgrimage ever since. When Alfred, Lord Tennyson came to Lyme, he was more interested in seeing landmarks connected with Jane Austen's novel such as where Louisa Musgrove had fallen on the Cobb, than with real events such as the Monmouth Rebellion!

Fire again was a major problem in 1844 when a blaze destroyed a large portion of the old town including the fine old coaching inn, The George which stood in Coombe Street and another casualty was the original Three Cups which stood opposite the Assembly Rooms. Even allowing for this destruction some good came out of it for some of Lyme's most dilapidated and squalid tenements were also consumed in the conflagration.

Some of the older industries in Lyme such as the cloth and lace trade, really no more than cottage industries, were beginning to disappear. Others briefly took their place; quarrying off the shore for Blue Lias (this continued unabated until 1914 and had the unfortunate effect of worsening the coastal erosion) and a bit later a cement works was set up on Monmouth Beach; that too continued up until the outbreak of the Great War.

More and more, tourism became the major industry in Lyme and once the town acquired its own railway station then the stage was set for a great influx of visitors. Not just holidaymakers in general, but artists and writers migrated here for their inspiration. Lyme's literary connections are fairly well known and include Sir Francis Palgrave; GK Chesterton who holidayed in the town and stayed at the Three Cups, Beatrix Potter, and JRR Tolkien who visited Lyme when a youth and later returned many times with his wife and children. PG Wodehouse set some of the plot of ,'Love Among the Chickens' in a thinly disguised Lyme and Geoffrey Household set a major part of his most well known novel, 'Rogue Male' in and around Lyme Regis. John Fowles's highly acclaimed novel, 'The French Lieutenant's Woman' was set, written and later filmed in Lyme. John Fowles was a resident of the town and became the curator of the museum. The literary tradition of Lyme has not died away; more recently, Colin Dexter set the opening of one of his Inspector Morse novels in Lyme, having Morse as a guest in the Bay Hotel on Marine Parade. Tracy Chevalier, the bestselling novelist, set a recent novel in the town, 'Remarkable Creatures,' dealing with aspects of Mary Anning's life. This tradition shows no sign of abating.

Lyme Regis is a small town in size and in population (which has scarcely tripled in five hundred years). It has nowhere to go, but equally, nothing to prove. It is static, yet ever-changing and evolving. It lives in the present, yet rejoices in and celebrates its past.

Yes, it is a *small* town, but for those who live here, for those who visit here too, it is a *great* town.

****

Of necessity this has been a brief overview of Lyme Regis and omits far more than has been included and my thanks go to those who know or knew far more than I about this town of ours;

John Fowles, Rodney Legg, John Lello, Maggie Lane, Jo Draper Nigel Clarke and the 'father' of them all, George Roberts all of whose works I consulted and they are heartily recommended for those wishing to know more.

Lyme Regis, Lyme Regis

Lyme Regis, Lyme Regis...

There is a magic about the place.

An aura, an atmosphere which pervades the air

and seems to cling to the fabric of each building

a sense of being, a sense of history, a sense of permanence.

The houses tumble dizzily towards the sea,

as though they are in motion.

And when they reach the sea,

there is a challenge to be met,

questions to be asked

inviting the sea to do its worst

which it can do......and.....yet,

the sea has never quite held mastery

over the town and its people.

And although the mortal remains of those that have loved and lived here

have crumbled and returned to dust,

their spirit and love of Lyme lives on

their phantoms and shades are sensed and heard

as quiet footsteps echoing through the ancient lanes,

seen as fleeting shadows out of the corner of the eye

and heard as half caught conversations carried on the breeze.

Lyme says, "Love me and I will love you back"

And you do. For it is so.

The Return

If I were to return to Lyme one day,

the same soul,

a different body.

Would I remember?

Would the beauty of the past,

coincide with the beauty of the present?

If I were to return to Lyme one day,

the same soul,

a different body.

Would I remember?

Would the love of my past,

conflict with the love of my present?

If I were to return to Lyme one day.

the same soul

a different body

Would my soul remember?

and say once again,

this is home?

****

Acknowledgements:

My grateful thanks once more to Gill, who spent many more hours in the company of Sherlock Holmes than she could possibly have wished for and did her best to keep me on that grammatical straight and narrow once more. Hopefully she succeeded, but any mistakes of any nature whatsoever are mine alone as much as I may wish to blame someone else!

Thanks to friends in Lyme Regis, some of whom find themselves within these pages!

Thanks to family and friends who shouted encouragement from the sidelines and dashed on the field with half-time oranges or bought the occasional cider. This is for all of them and especially Duncan, Melody, Donna, Corin, Louise, Ayden, Kieron, Nikiah and Deryn.

And Lydia, who this time around did *not* get the last word!!

I am indebted to MX Publishing and their hugely supportive team of Holmes authors who are the very best in their field. My efforts seem quite puny and lightweight compared with theirs.

David Ruffle.

Links:

www.mxpublishing.co.uk

www.storiesfromlymelight.blogspot.com

www.holmesian.net

www.sherlockholmes.com

www.lymeregis.org

Also from MX Publishing

Close To Holmes

A Look at the Connections Between Historical London, Sherlock Holmes and Sir Arthur Conan Doyle.

Eliminate The Impossible

An Examination of the World of Sherlock Holmes on Page and Screen.

The Norwood Author

Arthur Conan Doyle and the Norwood Years (1891 - 1894) – Winner of the 2011 Howlett Literary Award (Sherlock Holmes book of the year)

www.mxpublishing.com

Also From MX Publishing

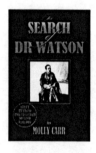

In Search of Dr Watson

Wonderful biography of
Dr. Watson from expert Molly
Carr – 2nd edition fully updated.

Arthur Conan Doyle, Sherlock
Holmes and Devon

A Complete Tour Guide and
Companion.

The Lost Stories of Sherlock Holmes

Eight more stories from the pen of John
H Watson – compiled by Tony
Reynolds.

www.mxpublishing.com

Also From MX Publishing

Watsons Afghan Adventure

Fascinating biography of Watson's time in Afghanistan from US Army veteran Kieran McMullen.

Shadowfall

Sherlock Holmes, ancient relics and demons and mystic characters. A supernatural Holmes pastiche.

Official Papers of The Hound of The Baskervilles

Very unusual collection of the original police papers from The Hound case.

www.mxpublishing.com

Also From MX Publishing

The Sign of Fear

The first adventure of the 'female Sherlock Holmes'. A delightful fun adventure with your favourite supporting Holmes characters.

A Study in Crimson

The second adventure of the 'female Sherlock Holmes' with a host of sub-plots and new characters joining Watson and Fanshaw

The Chronology of Arthur Conan Doyle

The definitive chronology used by historians and libraries worldwide.

Also From MX Publishing

Aside Arthur Conan Doyle

A collection of twenty stories from ACD's close friend Bertram Fletcher Robinson.

Bertram Fletcher Robinson

The comprehensive biography of the assistant plot producer of The Hound of The Baskervilles

Wheels of Anarchy

Reprint and introduction to Max Pemberton's thriller from 100 years ago. One of the first spy thrillers of its kind.

www.mxpublishing.com

Also From MX Publishing

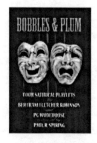

Bobbles and Plum

Four playlets from PG Wodehouse 'lost' for over 100 years – found and reprinted with an excellent commentary

The World of Vanity Fair

A specialist full-colour reproduction of key articles from Bertram Fletcher Robinson containing of colour caricatures from the early 1900s.

Tras Las He huellas de Arthur Conan Doyle (in Spanish)

Un viaje ilustrado por Devon.

www.mxpublishing.com

Also From MX Publishing

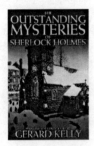

The Outstanding Mysteries of
Sherlock Holmes

With thirteen Homes stories and
illustrations Kelly re-creates the
gas-lit, fog-enshrouded world of
Victorian London

Rendezvous at The Populaire

Sherlock Holmes has retired,
injured from an encounter with
Moriarty. He's tempted out of
retirement for an epic battle with
the Phantom of the opera.

Baker Street Beat

An eclectic collection of articles,
essays, radio plays and 'general
scribblings' about Sherlock Holmes
from Dr.Dan Andriacco.

www.mxpublishing.com

Also From MX Publishing

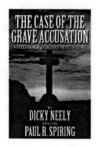

The Case of The Grave Accusation

The creator of Sherlock Holmes has been accused of murder. Only Holmes and Watson can stop the destruction of the Holmes legacy.

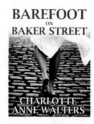

Barefoot on Baker Street

Epic novel of the life of a Victorian workhouse orphan featuring Sherlock Holmes and Moriarty.

Case of Witchcraft

A tale of witchcraft in the Northern Isles, in which long-concealed secrets are revealed -- including some that concern the Great Detective himself!

www.mxpublishing.com

Also From MX Publishing

The Affair In Transylvania

Holmes and Watson tackle Dracula
in deepest Transylvania in this
stunning adaptation by film director
Gerry O'Hara

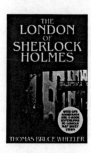

The London of Sherlock Holmes

400 locations including GPS co-
ordinates that enable Google Street
view of the locations around
London in all the Homes stories

I Will Find The Answer

Sequel to Rendezvous At The
Populaire, Holmes and Watson tackle
Dr.Jekyll.

www.mxpublishing.com

Also From MX Publishing

The Case of The Russian Chessboard

Short novel covering the dark world of Russian espionage sees Holmes and Watson on the world stage facing dark and complex enemies.

An Entirely New Country

Covers Arthur Conan Doyle's years at Undershaw where he wrote Hound of The Baskervilles. Foreword by Mark Gatiss (BBC's Sherlock).

Shadowblood

Sequel to Shadowfall, Holmes and Watson tackle blood magic, the vilest form of sorcery.

www.mxpublishing.com

Also From MX Publishing

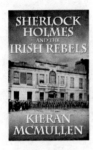

Sherlock Holmes and The Irish Rebels

It is early 1916 and the world is at war. Sherlock Holmes is well into his spy persona as Altamont.

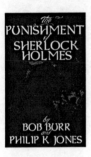

The Punishment of Sherlock Holmes

"deliberately and successfully funny"

The Sherlock Holmes Society of London

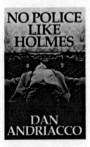

No Police Like Holmes

It's a Sherlock Holmes symposium, and murder is involved. The first case for Sebastian McCabe.

www.mxpublishing.com

Also From MX Publishing

In The Night, In The Dark

Winner of the Dracula Society Award
– a collection of supernatural ghost
stories from the editor of the Sherlock
Holmes Society of London journal.

Sherlock Holmes and
The Lyme Regis Horror

Fully updated 2nd edition of this
bestselling Holmes story set in Dorset.

My Dear Watson

Winner of the Suntory Mystery Award
for fiction and translated from the
original Japanese. Holmes greatest
secret is revealed – Sherlock Holmes is
a woman.

www.mxpublishing.com

Also From MX Publishing

Mark of The Baskerville Hound

100 years on and a New York policeman faces a similar terror to the great detective.

www.mxpublishing.com

Lightning Source UK Ltd.
Milton Keynes UK
UKOW040219040412

190085UK00001B/6/P